DEAD BEFORE DINNER

A MADDIE SWALLOWS COZY MYSTERY

KAT BELLEMORE

KB PRESS

ALSO BY KAT BELLEMORE

A NOTE FROM THE AUTHOR

Before *Dead Before Dinner* came to be, I had written nearly two complete small town romance series. *Borrowing Amor* is my first and takes place in New Mexico. The second takes place in the small Californian coastal town of Starlight Ridge.

I love both.

But mystery has been calling my name for some time. I'm especially drawn to mysteries that have quirky characters and make me just as invested in their lives as I am in solving the crime. Books like Richard Osman's *The Thursday Murder Club*, and TV shows like *Psych* and *Monk*, come to mind.

When making the decision to start writing cozy mystery, I knew I wouldn't be leaving romance entirely, and I also knew that I didn't want to leave my characters.

There is more to these towns and the people in them than first meets the eye.

Which is why you now get to experience these lovely towns from a completely different perspective. One that now includes murder and suspicion, in addition to light-hearted humor.

And the characters you knew and loved from the romance series? They are now side characters, helping my sleuth on her journey.

Dead Before Dinner is the first book in the Maddie Swallows mystery series. I hope you enjoy reading it as much as I had writing it. Because in writing mystery, I have found where my heart is.

Important Note: Your favorite characters do NOT die. Just in case you were worried.

1

My heart constricted, and I wished I knew what to say. "Yikes. That's rough. How does that make you feel?" I tried to keep the inner therapist from breaking free, wanting to come across more as an understanding friend, but it wasn't working.

"Mad," Lilly said, crossing her arms over her chest and slinking further down in her chair. "Upset. Livid. Like I want to run away from home and never speak to you again." She tossed me a glare for good measure.

I sucked in a long breath, counted to three, and slowly released it. Her reaction was natural. It wasn't personal.

"Have you been able to video chat with your friends lately? I know it's been hard since the move."

"Yes, and it only makes it worse."

"Because you hear about what you're missing out on? I

know that has to be really difficult. What if I gave you a challenge to—"

"Don't treat me like one of your patients, Mom," Lilly said, standing from the kitchen chair. "You dragged me away from Albuquerque to live in a town that's so small, no one even knows it exists. I gave up my friends. My life. Dad." Her voice hitched on that last part. "And you think a couple of shrink sessions will make it all better. You really want to help me? Try getting back together with Dad. Maybe you two could get a therapist of your own. That seems like the kind of thing that's right up your alley. But don't pretend you care about me—like you want to help. If you did, we'd have spent Christmas together last week. As a family."

I sat at the table, a bowl of melting ice cream sitting in front of me. I'd known Lilly was struggling with the divorce. And the move. It wasn't easy for a sixteen-year-old girl to have her life uprooted like that. But I'd thought she'd be doing better by now—would have adjusted more. Her brother certainly had. Of course, as long as Flash had access to a computer, he was happy.

It was harder for a teenage girl, though. And she was right. Christmas should have been spent together as a family. Their father had canceled at the last minute because of an unexpected snowstorm up north, and he'd felt terrible about it. But Lilly had pointed out that if her father and I hadn't gotten a divorce, we would have been trapped together, rather than apart.

I'd invited her down to the kitchen for ice cream, hoping that would soften her up for a little heart-to-heart, but her ice cream sat untouched, and our relationship seemed worse than ever.

In a last-ditch attempt, I said, "I heard that one of the seniors at your school—Kim Darby's daughter—is throwing a New Year's Eve party. Wouldn't hurt to go check it out. You might find that there's more to this town than first meets the eye."

Had we still been in Albuquerque, there would be no way I'd ever allow my daughter to go to a party of any kind. This was different, though. We were in Amor, New Mexico. Where nothing remotely interesting ever happened. And I was desperate.

Lilly snorted. "Nice try, Mom. I'm going to call Dad and ask him to drive down here and pick me up. I want to spend New Year's Eve at home. With my real friends."

And then she grabbed her jacket off the back of the chair, slipped her phone into the pocket, and stormed out the front door, brushing past my best friend, Trish, as she went. Trish stood on the front porch, a large bag of cat food in her arms and an expression of bewildered amusement on her face.

"You tried to have another talk with her, didn't you?" Trish eyed the bowls of melting ice cream on the table as she shut the front door and set the bag down. She seated herself in front of Lilly's bowl. "Don't mind if I do."

I rubbed a hand over my face. "Yeah. *Tried* being the

operative word there. Lilly is never going to forgive me. She's probably out there filming her video diary, creating a permanent record of what an awful mom I am."

"She'll be okay once she sees how many people need you here. I bet you anything that once we hang that OPEN sign for our therapy office, we'll have a wait list the length of the Rio Grande." Trish paused. "Of course, don't tell your mom that. She'll raise our office rent, considering what a good deal she gave you."

My mom had felt bad for me, wanting to give me a leg up after the divorce. But honestly, I was excited for this new adventure, and I didn't think I could ever go back to the university life, even if my ex-husband weren't the department head.

"I'll feel too guilty not to. We're paying half of what her previous tenants were." I shot Trish a glance. Her previously pink hair was now bleached and streaked with blue. "I like what Debbie did with your hair."

Trish ran a hand through her long hair. "Didn't think someone who ran a salon from her kitchen would have the skills I was looking for."

I managed a smile. "She always had skills, even when we were in high school."

Trish licked the last of the ice cream from her spoon, then nodded to my bowl and raised a questioning eyebrow.

I laughed and pushed it toward her. "Yes, you can have it." It was a blessing having Trish here, and she could have all the ice cream she wanted. I didn't know what I would have done if she hadn't agreed to move down to Amor with me. We'd both left tenured positions at a university a few hours north, neither under pleasant circumstances, and were both looking for a new start. She'd even agreed to be roommates with me, a single mom of two kids. That was true friendship. Of course, the cat she'd brought along for the ride—that was a different story.

Speaking of which, where was she?

I cast an uneasy glance around the kitchen. No flicker of a tail. No sounds of scratching.

I was safe for now. Probably.

Having Trish here with me was worth the anxiety her feline companion invoked. Not only did we live together, but we also worked together, co-owners of Amor Therapeutic Services. Not very creative, I could admit. We had a temporary sign out front as we tried to figure out something better. But for now, it would do the trick. It told people who we were and that we were coming. We'd been working out issues with the various insurance companies, but it looked like our grand opening might happen as soon as the end of next month. Now that it was so close—so real —I was equal parts giddy and terrified.

"Oh, yeah, I almost forgot to tell you," Trish said, a drip of ice cream making its way down her chin. She swiped at it with the back of her hand. "Debbie is throwing a New Year's Eve dinner party on Saturday. You want to go?"

Panic clenched my stomach.

Here I was pushing Lilly to go to a party she didn't want to go to, and I was no better. I had never done well with social situations, and it had only gotten worse since moving back to Amor two months earlier. All these people I had grown up with who had never left—and me coming back, the divorcee. The single parent. The failure.

I could sense the judgment.

"I don't know, Trish. It doesn't feel right to leave the kids home alone on New Year's Eve. You should definitely go, though. I don't want you to miss out on my account."

Trish narrowed her eyes. "You turn down every invitation people offer, and they are starting to be offended. There's talk, you know. That you think you're too good for them, now that you've been at your fancy university. We've been here for nearly two months, and it's high time you put the record straight. These are our potential clients, you know."

She was right, of course.

"But what about the kids?" I asked weakly.

"Bring them along. I'm sure Debbie won't mind a couple of extra guests."

"Yeah," Flash piped up from the staircase. "She'll probably have way better food than the parties I go to. Grownups get all the good stuff." He was standing on the bottom step, his hair sticking out in multiple directions. It looked like he was just waking up. I looked at my watch. One o'clock in the afternoon.

I threw a look of amusement at Trish. "He'll eat all the

food before the guests have first crack at it. You know he will."

Flash gave a solemn nod. "It's true."

You'd never know just by looking at my scrawny thirteen-year-old that he could consume two pizzas and a tray of chicken wings in one sitting. There had been many times we'd visited Trish, and I'd had to run to the grocery store to restock her fridge. But wherever all that food went, it was fueling his brain power. That kid was smart. Too smart for his own good sometimes.

"Awfully late for you to just be waking up, isn't it?" I asked, raising a pointed eyebrow.

"Had to stay up late. There was an online coding competition. It was based out of Australia. Remember, I told you about it."

I remembered now that he'd mentioned it, but that had been a week ago, and he hadn't mentioned it since. "Oh, right. How'd it go?"

"I won. Of course. Prize was pretty good this time too. Ten thousand dollars."

Both Trish and I stared, our mouths hanging open. "Ten... Who were you competing against?" I yelped.

I had known he'd won a few hundred dollars here and there with these competitions. And I knew he was good at what he did—he was obsessed, really. Spent all his time holed up in his room. Every time I peeked in, his fingers were flying over the keyboard in a language only other coders would understand. Or hackers. I wasn't sure which my son was, and when I'd asked, he'd said there was a gray area between the two, but not to worry. He wasn't doing anything illegal.

So, at least there was that.

But ten thousand dollars. That was big-league.

Flash raised a shoulder. "People." That was typical Flash, vague one-word answers. Or maybe it was just a boy thing. He grabbed the half-full ice cream container from the freezer and a spoon from the drawer, then lumbered back up to his room.

As I watched his retreating back, I had the distinct feeling that I was losing my kids. They were slipping away. I knew raising teenagers had its challenging moments, that every parent felt that way, but I couldn't help but wonder if I'd accelerated it. Maybe if I'd just stuck things out with Cameron, just until the kids were old enough to be out on their own...

"It wasn't a mistake moving here. Neither was the divorce. Cameron didn't see you—the real you," Trish said, easily reading my thoughts. That was what I got for having another psychologist for a best friend. "And frankly, I'm not sure you see the real you either. That department head position should have been yours, not Cameron's. They needed new blood in the psychology department. Someone who wasn't so busy chasing book deals and TV slots that they gave up everything that really mattered. You would have been fantastic."

I knew Trish was right. She always was.

Didn't make it any easier.

I gave her a weak smile as I slid my chair back and stood from the table. "So, about this party—"

A flash of fur tore across the kitchen, taking my words with it as it disappeared under the table. Before I had time to react, a paw whacked my leg and a cat bolted back up the stairs.

New Year's. A time of renewal. Change. Fresh starts.

I certainly hoped that was true as I tugged on the hem of my favorite red dress. It was the one I always wore when I needed to make an impression. I swore it used to be longer, though. Now, it barely hit just above my knees.

A quick glance at my phone.

Four-thirty.

Party started at six.

Where was Cameron? He was supposed to be picking up the kids.

I moved into the bathroom for a quick glance into the mirror. Eyeliner wasn't smudged. Hair was decent. Teeth. I should brush my teeth. But when I moved to turn on the faucet, the handle snapped off in my hand.

"Seriously?"

Apparently, this home had been vacant for three years after the owner moved across country and couldn't find anyone who wanted to move to a small town where there were no jobs and gossip was exchanged like currency.

I wondered what other surprises I was going to find. Other than the rattlesnake den we'd discovered in the backyard the previous week. That had not been a good day.

When married, neither Cameron nor I had been particularly handy and had never learned to do things ourselves. My skills hadn't improved since the divorce, so I grabbed my phone to call the local handyman. Until I realized I had no idea who that was nowadays. Twenty years ago, it had been George Finley. But he was dead now. That was what happened when you were ninety-eight and still thought you could take stairs two at a time.

"Trish," I called down the stairs. "Do you know who the fix-it guy around here is?"

A pause.

"How would I know?" her disembodied voice yelled from somewhere in the house.

She wouldn't. It was my hometown, and I should be the one with all the answers.

But I'd been gone too long.

My mom. Of course. I dialed her number.

No answer.

I sent her a text instead.

"Cameron's here," Trish yelled up the stairs.

Somehow Lilly had managed to convince him to drive the three hours so she could attend a party with her friends. I wasn't happy about it, but they had worked it out before I'd had the chance to protest.

There had been a condition attached, though. Flash had to come too. Not to the party—Cameron knew me well enough to know that wasn't happening—but Cameron had said he wanted to spend time with his son. Said they didn't talk much anymore, and he wanted the chance to salvage their relationship.

It was funny. Cameron made more effort to spend time with his kids now that we lived across state than he ever had when we'd lived in the same house.

I could hear the complaining from both Lilly and Flash as I hurried outside. Lilly grumbling that she had to be stuck with Flash in the back seat for three hours, and Flash complaining that he had to go at all. It didn't matter that his dad had told him he could choose any restaurant he wanted for their New Year's Eve together. Flash was convinced that the food at our adult dinner party would be better.

"You two are going to have a wonderful time," I said, blowing them both kisses as I shut the rear car door. I turned my gaze on Cameron in the driver's seat. He looked good. More than good. Great. Like the divorce suited him. "Have them home no later than nine o'clock on Sunday."

He gave me a little salute. "Yes, ma'am." An appraising gaze. "Nice dress. You have a date or something?" Cameron said it casually enough, but there was a hint of annoyance beneath the question.

"Something like that." Never mind that Trish was my date.

He nodded and looked away, like that might be something that bothered him. But then he turned back to me with a megawatt smile. "Oh, I almost forgot. I'm going to be out of town for the next three weeks; I leave on Tuesday for a book tour. I'll miss my weekend visits, but I'll make up for it when I get back."

My fists tightened just slightly, and I forced them to relax. The way he said it—he wasn't just touching base or passing on information. He wanted me to remember how successful he was. Like he wanted me to know what I was missing out on. I forced a smile. "That will be just fine. I'm sure the kids will understand. I'll come up with something fun to make up for it. Maybe a trip to Carlsbad Caverns or something."

Cameron's smile dipped just slightly. "How's your therapy office coming along?" I was sure he meant it as a dig as his gaze took in the all-but-deserted road that ran through my neighborhood. But for reasons unknown, it had the opposite effect on me.

"My mom was right. This place needs a therapist, and there's more than enough business for two." I threw a grin his way, gave one last wave to the kids, and walked back to the house.

I wasn't going to give him the satisfaction of a second glance.

An hour later, Trish bounced down the stairs, looking stunning in an emerald green dress, which surprisingly didn't clash with the blue streaks in her hair. Her long hair hung over her shoulders in ringlets and was partially pulled back by a sparkly green butterfly clip.

I placed a hand on my hip. "Just when I think I've pulled out all the stops, you manage to do one better."

"That wasn't my intention." But the compliment made Trish's smile widen, and she gave a little spin. "I just want to make a good impression, you know. I really haven't made many friends here yet."

"Everyone is going to love you," I said, nudging her with an elbow.

Trish smiled. "We're about to find out."

"You're sure she said the party started at six o'clock?" I whispered. We stood on Debbie's front porch, but it seemed awfully quiet. Of course, folks in Amor rarely drove anywhere, so the lack of cars wasn't a great indication.

"Yeah. Six o'clock sharp. I mean, it's a dinner party."

True, but that still seemed early for a New Year's Eve dinner party. I glanced around. A woman with long auburn hair was walking up the street, and it seemed like she might be coming to join us, but then she continued past the house. Before she did, our gazes met, and there was instant recognition. Not on my part, but on hers. Like we might have gone to school together—she seemed about the right age—or maybe it was just the town gossip that had clued her in on who I was.

"Maybe we should have come fashionably late," I whispered.

Trish raised an eyebrow. "Making a good impression, remember?"

My gut clenched. I had been avoiding everyone in town for a reason. Unlike Trish, I wouldn't have the opportunity for a first impression. Everyone had already formed an opinion, and from the little I'd heard, it wasn't good.

I took a step back from the door, and Trish noticed. She gave me a reproving glance and quickly knocked on the door, not giving me the chance to retreat.

Debbie flung the door open, looking casual in a pair of tight jeans and a long black shirt that had sequins along the top. It fit perfectly with the pink bob that she was sporting. In high school, she'd seemed to have a different hair color every other month. Looked like things hadn't changed much while I was away.

"Oh, Debs, I think we're a bit overdressed." Rather than my red dress giving me confidence like it usually did, it now made me want to shrink until no one noticed me. If the town thought I was avoiding them because I thought myself too fancy—too good for them—what were they going to think now?

"Maddie Swallows, I was starting to think that you were a figment of your mother's imagination." And then Debbie wrapped me in a hug. She stepped back and gave me an appraising once-over. "You look gorgeous. Don't change a thing."

I appreciated Debbie's kindness. But I was embarrassed. I had dressed as if I were attending an academic dinner. When I'd worked for the university, a "dinner party" had always just been an excuse for members of the psychology department to show off and talk about what research we were doing in hopes that we would gain the respect of our colleagues rather than their scorn. Most of the time, it had been the latter.

That was nothing like what Debbie was trying to do with this dinner. Have friends over. Relax. Have fun. I had nearly forgotten what that was like. She opened the door wider and ushered us in, closing it behind me. The smell of hair chemicals assaulted my sinuses, and I had to keep myself from sneezing.

"Thank you," I said, trying to ignore my watering eyes. Looked like I wouldn't be getting a perm anytime soon, because I was pretty sure I was allergic to whatever was in the air. "You look amazing yourself. A lot has changed in the past twenty years, but not you."

Debbie tossed an expression of mock horror in my direction. "We don't speak of age like that around here, honey. Talking like that makes me feel old."

I laughed. "Well, if it makes you feel better, no matter

how much time passes, I'll always be older by a couple of years."

"That does make me feel better, thank you." Debbie gestured to Trish. "What do you think of my handiwork?"

Trish held her hands up, framing her face, then did a model-like spin as she showed off her new locks.

"You always did have a way with hair," I said. "Even as a teenager, you had all the girls at school lined up behind the bleachers at lunch, ready to take our money. You were so talented, armed with only a pair of scissors. You probably made a hundred dollars a week giving haircuts."

"Try a hundred dollars a day," Debbie said with a wicked smile. "I charged twenty dollars a haircut. Mrs. Bailey—you remember her, don't you? Dark hair, even darker soul, probably started cutting hair because she was one of the three fates from Greek mythology who used scissors to separate people from their souls. Anyway, she was only charging ten. And yet everyone at school came to me. Moms never could figure out why their daughters' hair never seemed to lengthen." Her smile morphed into a scowl. "Until the principal caught me and ratted me out."

Oh, did I remember Mrs. Bailey. And I had been one of those who had asked my mom for money for a haircut, told her Mrs. Bailey had raised her prices, then snuck off to Debbie's bleacher hair salon. Once my mom found out what I had been doing, rather than being angry like the other girls' moms, she'd continued paying for me to get my hair cut at Debbie's house. My mom said my hair had never looked so good.

"I'm surprised you don't have your own salon, Debbie," I said. "I mean, I know cutting hair in your kitchen saves on overhead costs, but you always talked about wanting your own place."

Debbie's scowl deepened. "I've been trying. But James Rodney owns the only available rental space that would work for a salon, and he refuses to rent it to me. I mean, honestly. What can the man have against a haircut?"

"Mrs. Bailey," I said, immediately knowing she was most likely behind it. "She's on town council with him, isn't she? Elected right before I moved, and from what my mom has told me, Mrs. Bailey and James Rodney have somehow managed to keep their thumbs firmly in town business ever since."

"I thought of that too. But surely Mrs. Bailey doesn't need the space for herself. She's nearly seventy and has arthritis in her fingers. What few haircuts she does nowadays are the worst thing I've ever seen. I mean, honestly, folks come out of her home looking worse than when they went in."

"Doesn't mean that she doesn't have influence."

Debbie gave a small nod. "Which is why I've invited both of them to the party tonight, among others on the town council."

My horror must have been evident because Trish leaned in and whispered, "Remember, first impressions."

But that did not extend to people like James Rodney and Mrs. Bailey. I didn't care what they thought of me.

"I know I should have been upfront with why I was hosting this party," Debbie said with a guilty expression, like she was genuinely sorry for it. She gestured for us to follow her out of the entryway and to a couch in the front room. "But I've tried everything to get on James's good side, and frankly, I don't think he has one. You're my last hope."

"Oh, my. You are desperate if you're counting on Maddie to win over town council," Trish said. She immediately clamped her lips shut, like she'd just remembered those first impressions she kept talking about.

"Trish is right," I said. "I don't know how I can help. It's not like I was ever a particular favorite of either Mrs. Bailey or James Rodney." My gaze swept the front room. "Are we the first to arrive?"

Color darkened Debbie's cheeks. "I may have asked you to come earlier than the others. I wanted to talk to you alone—you know, see if you might be able to say good things about what a real salon could do for the town. Whether James Rodney likes it or not, this town needs to progress. That's why I also invited Mayor Freedman and his girlfriend, Katie. She's from Denver. Figured she'd have a progressive viewpoint."

This was too much. First off, I wasn't used to Sam Freedman being referred to as "mayor." We were around the same age and had been friends in high school. Second, this was a setup. My first time going out into town and giving it a chance, and I was being used as a pawn.

"Why me, Debbie? I mean, honestly, I've heard the things that people are saying."

Debbie waved a hand through the air, like town gossip was inconsequential. Like it didn't have an impact on whether you got a rental space for your hair salon. I was lucky that my mom owned the office space that Trish and I were now renting. If she hadn't...well, I knew I wouldn't currently be sitting in Debbie's front room, let alone be back in Amor.

"They respect you, Maddie. Whatever they may say, you were accepted into a fancy university and became a professor, of all things. Your mom has never stopped talking about how proud she is of you. And frankly, we are too. We're just kind of funny about how we show it. And once folks start seeing you around town again, I'm sure their opinion on Amor Therapeutic Services will change too."

"What do you mean—"

"Of course she'll tell this James guy how much this salon would mean to the town," Trish said, swinging an arm around my shoulders, cutting me off. It seemed that Trish hadn't told me of all the gossip she'd heard. "Anything to help out the best stylist in town."

"Trish—" I said, a warning in my tone.

"Later," she whispered.

Debbie's whole body visibly relaxed. "That means so

much to me. Seriously. I've been fighting town council for two years on this thing, and I'm at my wits' end. If this doesn't work, I don't know what I'll do."

Her gaze landed somewhere behind me. The front window.

"Looks like you'll get the chance sooner than I anticipated. Mr. James Rodney and his charming wife are early."

3

"James. Kandy. I'm so happy you could make it."
Debbie's smile was faker than her bright pink hair,
and it didn't seem to have any effect on the town
councilman.

I watched from the front room as James gave a slow
nod. "It was kind of you to invite us. But the answer about
your hair salon is still no."

Debbie's smile faltered slightly, but she plastered it on
even brighter than before and said, "Oh, the salon has
nothing to do with your invitation to tonight's party. In
fact, I insist that we don't talk business. See, I like to have a
variety of people over for dinner so I can get to know them
better. This is just me wanting to be neighborly."

James Rodney glanced behind him. "Is that why Marci
Bailey just arrived, with the mayor and his hooligan girlfriend not far behind?"

One of the things I had not missed while away was the small-town gossip. And yet I couldn't help but be intrigued. I pretended to not be too interested as I saw a shadow cross Debbie's expression.

"Katie is not a hooligan, and she's my guest."

James snorted and walked towards the dining room, dragging along his poor wife, who was mouthing *sorry* as they went.

He paused and looked back at Debbie. "Katie lied to every person in this town. And even after we found out the truth about who she was, you all act like you don't care. Like it doesn't matter. But people don't change, with rare exception." He threw a glance at me. "The ones who abandon where they came from, for instance."

"You talking about that Lawson girl?" a thin voice said from the doorway. "Changed her name to Swallows or something like that when she left."

Mrs. Bailey.

I pulled back, looking for a place to hide. I didn't need this right now.

"Maddie was always a troublemaker," Mrs. Bailey continued, her voice ringing through the house for everyone to hear. "It's a wonder she decided to come back at all. Left that poor husband of hers and ran off with the kids while at it."

My breath hitched, the pain of that decision sitting heavy on my chest. They didn't understand. No one did.

This was officially the worst New Year's Eve ever.

Trish rested a steadying hand on my arm, reminding me that there was one person who understood. Who had been with me through it all. But I didn't think that even Trish could get me through the night in one piece.

"Can we leave now?" I asked her under my breath.

"And leave Debbie to fight off those two all on her own?"

I didn't bring up that this was Debbie's own doing. I mean, the woman should have realized what would happen if she invited the most cantankerous members of town council to her "party." The whole thing had been set up to try to schmooze the least likely people to respond to flattery and food.

But Trish was right, so instead of running away, I stepped back, sat on the arm of one of the couches, and said in a loud voice, "Debbie, I love what you did with the place. I don't remember the miniature gnome collection. Did you start that after I left town?"

Silence fell upon the entryway, and Debbie stuck her head in. "Why yes, I did. Thank you for noticing." She then ushered in Mrs. Bailey. "You remember Maddie, don't you? And this is her friend, Trish. They are opening up a therapy office on Main Street. You might have seen the sign."

Mrs. Bailey's short, curly hair matched her round nose. Her short, plump stature did nothing for the effect, making her entire body seem the shape of a tomato. She pushed her glasses up the bridge of her nose and harrumphed.

"Yes. Your mother said you were back in town. Two months now, hasn't it been?"

Here we went. I supposed it was good to start with the worst of the lot first—everything would seem easy after this.

"Yes, ma'am. Just getting settled and trying to get everything in place for our grand opening. Should be accepting appointments within a month or so."

Mrs. Bailey fixed me under a hard stare. "And you think you're qualified to give folks in town advice, do you? Think you know how to *fix* us? Hard to help people you abandoned, though. People you left two decades ago. From the sound of it, it's become a bit of a nasty habit of yours. Leaving people, I mean."

I threw a pleading glance at Debbie. I was supposed to be helping her get her salon, but I was afraid I was only going to make things worse for her. And for myself.

Amazingly enough, it was James Rodney who stepped in. He must have been listening from just around the corner. "That's enough, Marci. The woman only came here tonight for a good time and to ring in the new year. Not to be put under interrogation for her life choices."

I stared, unbelieving. That was the nicest thing I'd ever heard James say. Hadn't known he had it in him.

"Besides, the woman has it hard enough," he continued. "This little therapy place of hers doesn't stand a chance, and as a single, unemployed mom, she's going to need all the sympathy you can muster."

And there it was.

"I think I need a drink," I said, hurrying from the room and their stares. As I went, I brushed past Sam and his girlfriend, who were standing in the entryway, like they didn't know if they were coming or going. Their gazes dashed to anywhere that I wasn't, as if they'd heard the entire conversation but didn't want me to know.

I did the same, wanting to pretend that the past fifteen minutes of my life hadn't happened. Moving toward the kitchen, I saw the dining room table was already set with the exact number of place settings needed for the expected guests, including name cards. Nine in total. Debbie had really outdone herself. Out of curiosity, I peeked to see where she had placed me.

Right between Mrs. Bailey and James Rodney. Of course. At least Sam and Katie were placed straight across the table. Maybe I could strike up a conversation with them and imagine that I wasn't sitting between two vipers.

"Water's in the fridge," a woman with platinum blonde hair said, following me into the kitchen. James's wife. "Kandy Rodney," she said, sticking out a hand.

I took it and shook it. "Maddie Swallows."

"Yes, I know. There's been a lot of talk about you around town lately." Her lips pulled into a slight smile. "Mainly what to do about you."

So much for escaping. I didn't know what to say—didn't want to engage in this conversation. Where was Trish when I needed her?

"That bad, huh?" My gaze took in the large kitchen. The chemical smell was worse in here, and it was making me slightly nauseous. I was sure the food would be amazing, but its aroma combining with the smell of the hair chemicals was not a good mix.

"Not at all," Kandy said. She opened the fridge and pulled out two water bottles, handing me one of them. "The mayor—Sam—has been trying to figure out ways the town council can help you get your office up and running quicker. It's not like we've had anyone qualified to practice psychology before—someone who can help the folks of this town in ways that we are lacking. If you ask me, Sam is doing it for Ruby, his sister. She's been a mess ever since...well, I'm sure you've heard her tragic story. Of course James is against it. He's against anything that doesn't benefit him." She lowered her voice. "Funny thing is, he's the one who could benefit from therapy the most."

"How do you mean?" I tried not to appear too interested. But this was James Rodney's wife, spilling info on what no one else would talk about. The problems that Amor faced. As a therapist, I needed to know what I was up against. Especially with people like James pretending they knew what was best for the town, refusing to take advice, and insisting on being in control.

Speaking of the man, James walked in from the dining room. "The woman said to be here at six-thirty, therefore we should eat at six-thirty. This is a dinner party, isn't it?

Kandy, you know my digestive system has a strict schedule."

"I'm sure we'll eat soon," Kandy said, her tone suddenly soft, like even she had to be careful around her husband. It only seemed to rile him up more.

"That's what you would think," James said, "but apparently the roast is taking longer than she expected, and it won't be ready for another thirty minutes. *Thirty minutes.* Last time I accept one of Debbie's invitations." He began lifting lids off pots that sat simmering, sniffed the contents, then replaced the lids. Next was the wicker basket that sat on the counter, a white linen cloth covering the contents. James peeked beneath, then pulled out a roll and snacked on it as he perused the rest of the kitchen. "Excuse me," he said, sliding behind me and opening the fridge. He rummaged for what felt like ages, then shut the door, emptyhanded.

Kandy shook her head, then gave me a look that seemed to say, *What am I going to do with him?* "Your digestive system can wait ten minutes for the appetizers," she told her husband. "But you know what that stomach of yours will think of the pastries—they're filled with cream cheese. Wait for the steamed vegetables."

He harrumphed, like he doubted the pastries would have any effect on him, but didn't press the matter further.

I'd assumed James Rodney must be the one in charge, his wife trying to keep up. That was how it had always felt for Cameron and me—I'd always been one step behind him. It seemed I had been wrong about them, though, and James probably didn't even realize how much influence his wife had over him. I liked that.

James left the kitchen, muttering about how if this was how Debbie planned on running her hair salon, she'd be out of business in the first month, and how could she expect him to take that kind of risk?

"You see why this place needs a therapist?" Kandy asked, opening the fridge her husband had just closed. She pulled out a tray that was filled with a variety of meats and cheeses, I assumed to go with the crackers that sat on the counter. I smiled and shook my head when she offered it to me—I could wait for dinner. Didn't want to fill up on cheese when I knew a roast was on its way.

Kandy took a few slices of each and returned the tray to the fridge. "Not only for people like my husband. Imagine this. You're venting to a friend about something or other, and what starts out to be someone sharing their feelings turns into gossip that's splattered on the local news by dinner time." She swallowed. "It's out of control, and the way I figure it, if people had someone other than their neighbor to vent to about the rough things going on in their lives, the town might look a lot different."

It wasn't all that bad, was it? "I know Amor had its share of problems back when I used to live here, but my mom seems to be under the impression that things are better than ever. That's how she got me to move back in the first place."

"That's because your mom is the type who makes good things happen. She is the one who spearheaded getting Sam into office, you know. She went head to head against town council. Against my husband. Sam is trying to change things around here. He really is. But he's up against some formidable opposition."

I thought on that as I took a pull from my water bottle. "How long have you lived in Amor, Kandy?"

"I moved here about four years ago. Didn't mean to stay, just visiting my sister. And then I met James." She paused, and a dark shadow crossed her face. It took a moment for it to clear, and her focus returned to me. "I'll be honest, ever since Mayor Freedman died—Sam's dad— I've wondered if it isn't time to move on. See what else the world has to offer. But James likes it here."

The accident. Even though I hadn't been in Amor for it, I'd heard plenty about it from my mom. Sam and Ruby's parents had been killed driving home from an anniversary getaway. And rather than let James Rodney become mayor, Sam had run against him. No one else had had the guts.

Thank goodness for Sam. I hated to think what things would be like if James were in charge.

Mrs. Bailey bustled in at that moment, looking flustered, with Debbie hot on her tail.

So much for hiding from the party.

"You should have gotten my input about the menu," Mrs. Bailey was saying. "I could have given you my specifications."

"And I already told you, I would have made the same dishes I'm serving you tonight, because I did my research."

Kandy and I exchanged raised eyebrows as Mrs. Bailey lifted the lid on one of the same pots James had just minutes before. "Smells spicy."

"Black pepper. Not too much, just enough to give it some flavor."

Mrs. Bailey then peeked into the garbage can, as if looking for evidence of what had gone into the food. "You're not exactly known in town for being a world-class cook."

Debbie's nostrils flared, and her eyes narrowed, but by the time Mrs. Bailey had glanced back, Debbie's expression had returned to neutral. "I do apologize for keeping you from dinner; you must be hungry. Why don't we head back to the dining room, and we'll start on the first course."

"You've been spending too much time with Miss Swallows here and her high-minded ways," Mrs. Bailey said. "We don't do things like *courses* here in Amor. I like all my food at once, the way God intended it. And on time." She turned to Kandy. "Don't you agree, Mrs. Rodney?"

Kandy nodded. "Yes, of course. And I know my husband would agree as well."

Well, that was a quick turnaround from the woman who had been ready to divulge all of Amor's secrets. Looked like she didn't like to ruffle Mrs. Bailey's feathers any more than the rest of us.

I wasn't sure that God intended for us to eat our meals one way or the other, but regardless, as if to prove a point that she could eat what she wanted, when she wanted it, Mrs. Bailey pushed past me and opened the fridge. She grabbed a puff pastry off a tray and then lumbered out of the kitchen as she shoved the entire thing into her mouth.

Mrs. Bailey stuck her head back in and threw a raised eyebrow in my and Kandy's direction. "Well, aren't you coming? I told you earlier there are things we need to discuss."

At first, I wondered if the cantankerous woman was speaking to me, but then Kandy hurried forward. "I really think I've said all I can on the matter."

Mrs. Bailey released a single barking laugh. "We'll see about that."

I watched the two women disappear into the dining room and turned to Debbie. "That woman is impossible. If Mrs. Bailey doesn't want you getting that rental space, do you really think I can do something to change her mind? I'm willing to try, but this is a difficult position you've put me in."

Debbie gave a resigned sigh. "I know. This was a terrible idea. The only thing she and James Rodney have done is insult my guests—my friends. I'm sorry I dragged you into this."

"Debbie," someone called from the other room.

The oven timer beeped. "I don't know if we're going to

make it to midnight," she mumbled as she moved to take the roast out. "I just want to make it through dinner."

"Debbie," they called again.

I handed her the oven mitts that sat on the counter, my stomach complaining of hunger. I hoped Debbie hadn't heard. "Want me to start cutting the meat, or would you rather I serve the soup and salad?"

She wrinkled her nose at the idea. "You are my guest, and I'm not going to make you work for your meal."

Except, wasn't that kind of what she'd done when asking me to work some influence with town council? Even so, had I known what Debbie was up to beforehand, I'd have still come to the party and tried to help her out. At least, I hoped I would have. Debbie had been right when she'd said we were friends. Twenty years hadn't changed that.

"You went to all this trouble, and I know it's not turning out how you'd hoped," I said. "It's the least I could do." My stomach growled again. Had I eaten lunch? I couldn't remember.

Debbie pulled the roast pan out of the oven as her name was once again called, this time with more urgency. "All right. You can help. But just this once." She threw me a grateful look as she hurried out of the kitchen to see what was so important. She hadn't been gone more than a few seconds when I heard a scream and a yell for someone to call Dr. Harris.

I dropped the knife I'd just picked up and rushed out

of the kitchen. It took me a moment to understand the horror that was written in the expressions of the rest of the dinner guests. Sam was leaning over something on the floor, his girlfriend standing several feet away, a hand covering her mouth, eyes wide.

He moved just enough for me to see Mrs. Bailey lying on the floor near the table, as if she'd fallen out of one of the chairs. I approached just in time to hear Mrs. Bailey whisper, "You said you'd done your research."

And then her body stilled.

I didn't need Dr. Harris to tell me that Mrs. Bailey was gone.

4

D ead. A woman was lying dead by the dining room table. And not just any woman. Mrs. Bailey. Debbie was asking anyone if they wanted something to eat while we waited for the doctor, but no one took her up on her offer. It was a little late for that.

I was actually starving, and the roast had looked amazing, as did the corn chowder. There was also a cranberry and sunflower seed spinach salad with raspberry vinaigrette that I'd been looking forward to trying.

Trish tapped me on the arm. "Would you stop looking at the kitchen? I'm hungry too, but you shouldn't make it so obvious."

I tore my gaze away from the kitchen. I hadn't even realized I'd been staring. "There's something wrong with me, Trish. I shouldn't be thinking about food. A woman just died, right in front of us. I've never seen a dead body before, but with Cameron always talking about serial killers, what if I've become desensitized? Maybe I no longer have a conscience."

Trish gave me an amused smile. "Nothing's wrong with the natural desire to eat—to survive. Everyone else is thinking it too, we just don't want to be the ones to admit it."

A knock on the door.

That had to be Dr. Harris.

Everyone froze where they were, all of us surrounding the table yet standing apart. Sam and Katie leaned against one wall, engaged in frantic whispering. When they caught me watching them, they both fell silent and turned away.

"Maybe someone should get the door," Trish said.

Debbie started, like she'd just realized that someone should probably be her. She moved from where she'd stood in the kitchen doorway.

As soon she'd turned the knob on the front door, Dr. Harris bustled in. He'd been fresh out of medical school when I'd left town, and it looked like he'd come into his own as he swept into the room with all the confidence that he'd lacked back then.

"I hear that Mrs. Bailey had a bit of a tumble," he said, scanning the room. "Where is the woman?"

I raised an eyebrow and looked to Debbie. Hadn't she told him what had really happened? She still seemed to be in shock and didn't make any move to correct the doctor.

"It was more than a little tumble," I said, taking a step toward Mrs. Bailey. We'd removed the place settings and used the tablecloth to cover her, none of us able to bear looking at the poor woman in the state she was in. It wasn't right. As much as we'd disliked her, she had been fierce and confident, never letting anyone, or anything, get in her way. And dying in this way... Well, she deserved better than being gawked at.

"Whatever it is, I'm sure I have just what she needs to feel right as rain." The doctor placed his hands on his hips as his gaze swept over the seven of us.

A sudden wave of nausea rolled over me. "Doctor, she's dead." The words felt sour, but someone had to say them. And it was true, even if no one wanted to face it. We'd just seen a woman die.

The doctor's face paled slightly. "Dead. Are you certain?"

I gestured toward the sheet that covered her figure. "You can check for yourself, if you'd like."

Dr. Harris took smaller steps now, no longer looking sure of himself. He was probably more used to things like bruises and broken bones. It wasn't like people didn't die in Amor, but considering we didn't even have a hospital, only a small clinic, most people did their dying in the big city.

He lifted a corner of the sheet and shifted Mrs. Bailey to better expose her face. He placed a finger on the side of her neck, as if looking for a pulse. "Yes, she's dead, all right." He released a heavy breath and straightened. "I suppose this means I should have driven my hearse."

I stared. "Your what?"

"Dr. Harris is also the mortician," Sam said, his voice faint. "Took on the position a couple of years ago."

"Yes, but most of my business is delivered from the hospital. I only need to worry about the preparation for the funeral and such, not... Well, let's just say it's rare that I stumble upon the dead in their natural habitat, if you know what I mean." Dr. Harris used his sleeve to wipe a bead of sweat from his brow and took a step toward the door, like he couldn't get out of there fast enough.

"Don't you think you ought to call the sheriff first?" Sam asked. "We don't yet know how Marci died."

Dr. Harris nodded slowly, thoughtful. "I already have my suspicions, but yes, you're absolutely right. I do need to call the sheriff." He stepped into the front room, supposedly to do just that.

James Rodney took a step backwards with Kandy. "Looks like everything is under control and we're no longer needed. Thank you for the invite to your party, Debbie. Do me a favor, and maybe don't invite us to the next one. Dead bodies and all. You understand."

Debbie looked like she was about to burst into tears. Not only was there no way she was getting her hair salon now, but I wondered if this would affect her business in general. She did cut hair in this very house, after all. In the very kitchen that sat only a few feet from Mrs. Bailey.

I glanced over at the shrouded figure. Dr. Harris hadn't covered Mrs. Bailey's face back up with the tablecloth. As I moved to replace it, there seemed to be something off about her—she didn't look right. Well, as not right as someone who was dead could look. Her lips were swollen, at least three times their normal size, and it looked like the rest of her face may have been well on its way.

"What are you doing?" Trish whispered, coming up behind me. "You look weird, checking out the deceased like that. First impressions, remember?"

"I think she had a reaction to something here," I murmured. "Look how swollen she is."

Trish forced herself to look at Mrs. Bailey, and she inhaled sharply. "I wish I hadn't looked, and I wish you weren't right. But that woman looks like a puffer fish. Why didn't the doctor notice?"

"I did," Dr. Harris said, stepping up from behind us. "I just talked to the sheriff, and everyone stays put until law enforcement gets here."

James and his wife were already halfway out the door when Dr. Harris made this announcement, and they looked like they might not heed his direction. But Kandy placed a hand on her husband's arm .and glanced back toward us, like she was telling him they might want to stay. He released a long sigh and gave in, retreating into the room.

And then we waited.

. . .

It wasn't Sheriff Andersen who arrived at the door as I had expected, but a woman. She wore a badge and a stern expression, moving around the room, frowning at us all, like she owned the place. I had the distinct feeling that we were guilty until proven otherwise.

"I know most of you, but not all," she said, her gaze lingering on Trish and me for a beat longer than the others. "I'm Sheriff Potts."

Her tone was gruff, and that stare—it was enough to get me to admit to the murder just to get out from under it. I shared a concerned look with Trish. There was no way this was going to go well. I was just grateful the kids hadn't come with us like I'd originally planned.

"Who owns the home?" Sheriff Potts barked. I didn't blame Debbie for not wanting to raise a hand and confess that it was she who had hosted the party. When she didn't answer right away, Sheriff Potts folded her arms over her chest, seemingly trying to appear as menacing as possible. It worked. "Well?"

Debbie finally found her voice, her pink hair seeming to have lost some of its luster since Mrs. Bailey had died in her dining room. "Me. It's my home."

"And you made all the food yourself?" Sheriff Potts asked, pulling a pad of paper from her pocket.

Debbie started to shake her head, but then shared a look with Kandy, and it morphed into a nod. I couldn't decipher Kandy's expression, but I could have sworn it was a warning. "Yes, ma'am. I prepared the food."

Sheriff Potts walked over to the deceased and pulled back the sheet, studying Mrs. Bailey before talking into a radio that hung on her hip. A man appeared and immediately started to take pictures.

"I'll be interviewing you each separately about what happened here, and no one leaves until I'm satisfied," she said.

"Excuse me, Danielle," Sam dared to say, stepping forward, with Katie shrinking behind him. She didn't look like she wanted to be noticed by the police, or anyone else for that matter. Hadn't spoken a word all night.

Sheriff Potts narrowed her eyes at the mayor's informal use of her first name but didn't say anything.

"I don't understand the need for the theatrics," he continued. "Are you saying Marci died under suspicious circumstances?"

"That's what I'm here to find out, Mr. Mayor." Sheriff Potts stepped closer to him than seemed necessary. "Were you aware of any allergies the deceased may have had?"

"Of course. Everyone was. A year ago, she accused me of trying to kill her because we had a salsa contest at our Christmas festival. The food, of course, not the dance. Marci was deathly allergic to nightshade vegetables—all nightshades. Tomatoes, bell peppers, potatoes, even chili powder. But we had other options at that Christmas festival, and it wasn't like she'd accidentally dish herself out a helping of chips and salsa."

"But you're saying she could have accidentally dished

herself out a helping of those nightshades here, this evening."

"Now, wait a minute," James bellowed from across the room. "We all arrived between six and six-thirty, yet it was after seven o'clock and we hadn't even been served our appetizers yet. No one had eaten." He threw an accusatory glare in Debbie's direction, as if he resented this fact.

He seemed to have forgotten the roll he'd snuck while scavenging, but I wasn't about to bring it up.

Trish lowered her voice so only I could hear. "Do you think it could have been poison?" She threw a nervous glance toward the sheriff. "Is there one that could make it look like a reaction? I doubt Mrs. Bailey was allergic to anything here. I heard her grilling Debbie about it several times—couldn't have been accidental."

Poison.

Now we were going from an accidental death to murder.

I didn't like the direction this night was going in.

It was bad enough merely being present for a death. But to think that one of us in this room could be a murderer... Well, that was the type of thing Cameron thrived on. This would have been the best dinner party he'd ever attended.

I didn't have my ex-husband's taste for the macabre, though.

My stomach felt sick. I thought I might throw up but didn't dare leave the room to do so.

"I know that no one liked her, with the exception of James Rodney," I whispered to Trish. "But honestly, murder? Amor has had its problems, but violent crime is not one of them."

"Maybe someone got tired of dealing with her insults. Couldn't take it anymore."

I just couldn't imagine anyone in that room doing something so awful.

"You've spent too much time talking with Cameron about his research, haven't you?" I said, watching the sheriff as she walked the room. "In spite of what my ex-husband might think, not everyone is a murderer. Although when you spend all your time talking to killers and studying their psyches, I can understand why he might think so."

Sheriff Potts raised her voice to be heard above the anxious whispers that had broken out. "I'm going to speak with each of you in the front room. When your turn is finished, you are free to go. But don't leave town. I need each of you accessible in case I have additional questions."

The sheriff then told Debbie she'd need a sample of everything she had meant to serve to us that evening, nodding to her deputy, who held evidence bags.

The hair stylist burst into tears. "My food is fine. I swear. Everything made according to recipe."

Sheriff Potts gestured to the front room. "It seems that you're the best one to start things off."

Debbie followed the sheriff, and by the time they were

finished, Debbie had been reduced to a blubbering mess, her eyes swollen from crying.

Trish hurried forward and wrapped an arm around Debbie's shoulders.

I moved toward the kitchen. "I'll get you some water."

"I don't think so," Sheriff Potts said. The deputy stopped me with an arm across the kitchen doorway. "Don't need you tampering with evidence. Tell me, Mrs..."

"Ms.," I corrected her. "Swallows."

The sheriff nodded. "Tell me, Ms. Swallows, where were you at the time of Mrs. Bailey's death?"

My breath hitched.

"Well?"

"In the kitchen, helping Debbie. But I don't see why it matters. Her death was accidental—something ended up in the food that we didn't know Mrs. Bailey was allergic to."

Sheriff Potts settled her gaze on me, unflinching. "Sure. That's a possibility. Except, the host of this party claims she took extra precautions to make sure that nothing made it into the food that shouldn't have been there. Said she was asked about it several times by the late Mrs. Bailey. 'Micromanaged' is the word she used." The sheriff stepped closer. "It seems, Ms. Swallows, that you spent a considerable amount of time in the kitchen prior to the death. The closer I look at this, it looks a lot less like an accident and a lot more like murder." She paused. "If you are wondering, yes, you, along with the others, are all suspects. And from where I'm standing, you're what I like to refer to as a strong suspect."

5

"Strong suspect. That's what she referred to me as," I said, pacing the house. I was too worked up to sit still and eat the waffle breakfast that Trish had whipped up, even though it smelled amazing.

So much for a fresh start. I was starting the new year as a murder suspect.

"I doubt she really believes that," Trish said, shoveling a forkful of waffle into her mouth. "I know I brought up the possibility of poison and all that last night, but I really just think the old lady keeled over and died. Seriously. She had too many allergies and too much stress in her life."

"Maybe. But you saw her, all swollen like that." I blew out a frustrated breath and raked my fingers through my hair. "Just before we left, Sheriff Potts said she'd been asking about me. Said she'd heard that I'd recently moved back to town, kept to myself. Like that was a bad thing. But that's not a motive to kill someone. Who did she ask, anyway, James Rodney?"

I pulled in a shuddered breath. It was happening all over again. At the university, I had been under suspicion for theft, as had Trish, Cameron, and the rest of the psychology department.

The strain of having to prove myself, and then suspecting the same things of those closest to me, had been too much. I had lost everything because of it. I couldn't go through that again. And yet, here I was. Except, rather than others thinking of me as a thief, they'd done one better.

Murder.

My phone burst into song, and I glanced at the screen. "My mom." Since I'd moved back to Amor, she had either called or visited at least twice a day. I supposed as a single older woman, she didn't have a lot to do, and the kids and I provided a nice distraction.

But I wasn't in the mood to chat. Not with—

The doorbell rang.

Trish and I shared an anxious glance.

"When are you expecting the kids back?" she asked.

I slipped my phone back into my pocket. "Not until late afternoon. And they wouldn't ring the doorbell."

I stood, knowing who must be on the other side of the door. But I had nothing more to say to that woman. The sheriff knew everything I did—probably more.

When I flung the door open, I intended to tell her all of that. But it wasn't Sheriff Potts who greeted me.

"If you wanted to see me, you could have just stopped by and said hi. No need to break your faucet to do it."

A tall man stood on my porch, the start of a beard not quite hiding his strong jawline. A baseball cap covered whatever mop lay under it, but there were those eyes—bright blue and laughing. And that nose. Just slightly too big for his face, and yet it fit him perfectly.

"Benji!"

I found myself being swept off my feet, flung through the air, and then plopped back onto my feet.

"I'm serious, you should have stopped by," he said, leaning against the doorframe.

Honestly, I hadn't realized he still lived in town. Figured he'd have gone off and married his high school sweetheart, leaving this place in the dust. We'd both had big dreams of escaping. Apparently he hadn't followed through with his.

"I know. But things have been a bit...intense lately."

"Aw, yes, the disgraced psychologist-slash-murderer. Once again, if what you needed was an adventure, you could have just asked. I would have come up with something." Benji tossed a smile at me, one that I knew well. One that I couldn't help but return. And one that I had desperately needed.

"Anyone want to introduce me to the hottie?" Trish asked from somewhere in the background.

Trish. I had completely forgotten she was there.

I stepped back, willed the heat in my cheeks to dissipate—though I wasn't certain it had listened—and said, "Trish, this is Benji. We met in preschool and were inseparable for the next fifteen years. Well, mostly. His girlfriends didn't love when I tagged along on their dates."

"And then you moved across the state, and I haven't heard from you since," he reminded me, not that I needed it. I had always felt guilty that we'd lost touch—that I hadn't known what had happened to him. Life had gotten busy in the big city, and my aspirations had taken over. When working on my PhD, it was the only thing I had thought about from sunup to sundown. And then Cameron and the kids had happened... I had never been short on excuses.

I lifted a shoulder. "Whatever happened to you running away to California and becoming famous? No one could strum a guitar the way you did."

"Is that all it was to you?" Benji gave a dramatic eye roll, but he was smiling. "I didn't just *strum* the thing, you know. I rocked it. You do know that's how I got the girlfriends I had in high school. Every one of them."

I laughed. It was so true. Otherwise, the poor guy never would have managed to get himself a date. He had been scrawny and ridiculously awkward at the time, nothing like he was now. I noticed he'd bulked up in the past two decades.

"So, why didn't you go? Did you manage to snag a wife

with your guitar as well?" I teased. "Surely she would have realized at some point that yes, you can play, but your singing sets off car alarms."

Benji's smile dipped just slightly, but it quickly returned to its full wattage. "Never mind my singing. I promise I won't serenade you anytime soon. Will you show me which faucet you need replaced? I need to head over to the Rodneys' house after this. Something about a faulty outlet in their kitchen."

This hadn't been a social call? Benji, the man who had been able to do calculus and answer every one of our teacher's questions correctly, while simultaneously doodling and daydreaming of being a famous guitarist, was a handyman. He fixed faucets and outlets for a living. He'd never left. And, from what I could tell, never married.

"I'll show you where Maddie managed her feat of strength," Trish said, as I attempted to gracefully recover from my shock. "And I don't mind saying that guitar strumming doesn't do a thing for me, so you might want to pick up another skill."

"What does do it for you?" he asked, following her up the stairs, his tone amused.

Trish paused and turned back. "This is where you're supposed to be offended and want to prove me wrong. You pull out your guitar and give me the best you got, and then I realize that yes, that is all it takes to sweep me off my feet. And then we live happily ever after."

"Ignore her," I called up. "And forget the guitar. She hasn't met a decent guy in a while, and at this point, showing up is all it takes."

Trish threw me a playful scowl, then proceeded the rest of the way to the second-floor bathroom.

My bathroom. It was a disaster. I hadn't expected company. Hopefully I'd at least put my bra into the hamper.

How had Benji known about the broken faucet in the first place? I hadn't told anyone—didn't even know who to call.

Except.

"Mom," I groaned with a shake of my head. I was grateful I'd have a working faucet, but a heads up would have been nice.

Speaking of which, why hadn't my mom told me Benji was the new handyman? Or even that he still lived in town? Surely this was something worth sharing, considering how close Benji and I had been.

My mom was funny like that. She was the biggest gossip in town, but there were times she was very selective in which information she shared. She liked the control—liked playing God. At least, that was how it had always seemed to me.

Apparently, this was one of those times when she'd decided to restrain herself and keep quiet.

"Benji," I said as he finished cleaning up from his

repair. "You mentioned earlier that you knew about the incident from last night. What exactly are people saying?"

As shocking as Mrs. Bailey's death was, the news had probably been spreading around town before Trish and I had even left Debbie's house.

Benji didn't respond right away as he zipped up his tool bag. "That her death was suspicious," he finally said, throwing me a glance. "There were eight of you who attended this dinner party that the rest of us weren't invited to, and only seven came home. The town is betting it was either you, Debbie, or Katie. Although, my money is on James. He's probably the only one who has it in him."

My mouth moved, but nothing came out. People were making bets? Whether figurative or literal, it didn't matter. There were people in the town who thought I was capable of killing someone—that my leaving town to pursue my dreams equated with being a coldblooded murderer.

I wasn't the only one they suspected, though, which said a lot about the trust within the town, even between those who had stuck around.

Benji must have been able to see the horror on my face because he quickly added, "It's just idle chatter. No one actually believes it. Just something to talk about."

"Well, then, they need to find a new subject," I said, my tone harsher than I'd intended.

"I agree." Benji blew out a breath and raked one hand through his hair. "Look, I'll keep my eyes open, okay? And ears. The thing is, I spend time in the homes of every person who was at that party. And on a regular basis. If the town gossip is correct, and Mrs. Bailey's death was not an accident, that means..."

"That on a regular basis, you are spending time with a murderer," I finished for him.

6

I plastered on the best smile I could muster. The kids could not know about what had gone on at that dinner party. They'd been through so much already, this was the last thing they needed. Their mother, a murder suspect. And if Cameron ever decided he wanted full custody, I could bet how the judge would look at that.

"Mom," Flash yelled, jumping out of Cameron's car before it had come to a complete stop. He ran over and gave me a big hug. He was so smart and beyond his years in many ways, but he was also still my baby. My Flash. And I hoped he wouldn't grow out of it. "Did you save leftovers from your party? You promised you'd save leftovers."

I tried to keep my smile in place. "Sorry, buddy. There were no leftovers. But how about pizza for dinner?"

His eyes widened, his expression a mixture of shock and awe. "Mom, how much did you and Trish eat? Did you eat an entire tray of chicken wings by yourself? That would be awesome if you did."

I laughed and ruffled his hair. "Not this time. I think I need some more practice."

"I don't mind teaching you." And then he waved goodbye to Cameron and lugged his overnight bag inside.

Lilly was less enthusiastic when she stepped out, her expression indecipherable. Her gait was slow, but her eyes —I swore they held relief. Like she was glad to be home. But that was probably wishful thinking.

"Hey, how did it—"

But Lilly had already walked past me and into the house. So much for that.

Cameron folded his arms across his chest and leaned against the car. "I don't understand girls, Maddie. Especially teenage ones. She wanted to come up to the city so bad, but then she was ornery the entire time. Locked herself in her room and wouldn't come out. When Flash stays in his room, it's different. He's not mad. And he'll at least come out for food."

Welcome to my life.

I knew I should act at least a little sympathetic, but I couldn't help but feel a little vindicated, remembering all the times Cameron had been gone, never making me and the kids a priority, and therefore never understood what it was truly like to be a parent of teenagers.

I raised a shoulder and gave him a look that I hoped conveyed, *What are you going to do?*

Cameron furrowed his brow. "Come on, Maddie. I'm drowning here."

"Well, when did her attitude change? On the drive up? Before the party? After the party? This morning?" Even if the man did drive me crazy, I did want to help him have a relationship with his kids. They needed it. As did he.

Cameron took a moment to think on it. "After the party. I picked her up early. She was quiet. Went to her room and barely came out again until it was time to drive back here."

What seemed obvious to me still didn't seem to have registered with the man. "Don't you see, something happened at that party with her friends. This move has been very difficult for her."

"But it's only been a couple of months since she's seen them. How much could have changed in that short amount of time?"

The man really did need help. "With teenage girls? A lot. When I was—"

I stopped when I saw that Sheriff Potts had parked her squad car a couple of doors down and was walking in our direction. And she was looking straight at me.

"When you were what?" Cameron asked.

Panic settled in. Cameron couldn't know about this, not when I didn't know if it was something he would use against me in the future. I didn't want to give him the chance. "You know what, I just realized I have dinner in the oven. But thanks for bringing the kids back home.

Have fun on your book tour. Send a postcard." I practically shoved the man back into his car.

"You know, I just drove three hours," he said, frowning as he put on his seatbelt, "and I won't see the kids for nearly a month. I know we aren't married anymore and all that, but you could still invite me in for dinner. I'd love to see what you've done with your new home."

The thought made me cringe. I never wanted to receive, or give, a dinner invitation ever again.

"I know, and normally I would. But now's really not a good time." I tried to appear calm, even as I threw a panicked glance in Sheriff Potts' direction. "Have a safe drive."

I spun away from the car just as the sheriff approached. It wasn't more than a few seconds later that Cameron peeled away from the curb, apparently not caring that he was speeding away at twice the limit, even as the sheriff watched.

"Boyfriend of yours?" Sheriff Potts asked, her gaze focused on the car, almost like she was memorizing the license plate number.

"Ex-husband."

Sheriff Potts turned to me, seeming surprised, but she quickly masked it. "I have more questions for you."

"I figured you would. But I've told you everything I know."

"You haven't told me why you are here in Amor. I know what everyone is telling me, but what I want is the real story. I can't bring myself to believe half of what the people in this town are saying."

People in this town. Meaning, Sheriff Potts wasn't originally from Amor. I wondered how long she'd lived here.

Sheriff Potts raised an eyebrow, prompting me to answer her inquiry. Tell her why I was in Amor.

"Not to kill anyone, if that's what you're implying."

The sheriff studied me, and I forced myself to hold her gaze. My family situation was none of the sheriff's business, and I planned on keeping it that way.

"You must know that your being here does raise some questions," Sheriff Potts finally said. "You left a successful career. A long marriage. Withdrew your kids from school and moved across the state. For what? Seems like something of a midlife crisis. Maybe you've been on the edge for a while now. You had to escape it all."

"You don't know any—" I started to say, but the sheriff pressed on.

"That doesn't explain what you're doing back in Amor, though. Why not transfer to a different university? Why give up an illustrious career? Did something happen that made it so you wouldn't be hired by another university? Or was it simply that you came back to be closer to your mother?"

The questions buzzed around me, closing in. I shook my head, but the sheriff kept talking. Kept asking things I didn't want to talk about.

I couldn't take it anymore, being bullied into submission, and I snapped.

"I could ask you the same thing, Sheriff Potts. About what you are doing here," I said, attempting to hold her gaze as her eyes narrowed. It wasn't easy to do. But I was the psychologist here, not her. I was the expert in reading people—in getting people to talk. "You're obviously not from Amor. You act hardened and tough, as if you received your training in a rough place. You're overcompensating. Trying to prove you are good at your job, that a woman can be just as good a sheriff as a man, even though you really needn't go to so much trouble. The sheriff that came before you didn't do much except play chess at the park. We knew where to find him if we needed anything, but he didn't even have a deputy. Which is why I'm very interested in why you are here. This isn't the type of place you go to further your career—it's the type of place you come to end it."

Sheriff Potts' nostrils flared slightly, but that was the only indication that I'd hit a nerve. She was very good at controlling her external emotions—not letting anyone see what was going on under that armor she'd created for herself.

"I'm not here to be psychoanalyzed, Mrs. Swallows."

"Ms. Swallows, if you don't mind."

Sheriff Potts broke eye contact and made a note in her pad. "You left your big university job to open a therapy office in a town where no one seems to want one. I'm not the only one full of contradictions."

That gave me pause. "What do you mean no one wants it? Sam does. I heard that he was trying to arrange it so I could open up sooner—wanted to give me any support he could."

"Uh-huh." The sheriff made another note on her pad. "Did Mayor Freedman tell you this himself? Or give any indication that this was the case?"

I froze when I realized that no, he hadn't. It had all been based on gossip. Words that had spread through the grapevine via Kandy. And I was just now realizing that the message might have been drastically altered on its way from point A to point B. If there had been any message at all.

Because if he really had been that desperate to help me, wouldn't he have talked to me directly rather than everyone other than me?

"I'm sure he was getting around to it." My words held no conviction.

Sheriff Potts flipped to a previous page in her notepad. "According to some, you are, and I quote, 'a meddlesome woman who has come back because she failed in her marriage and is seeking validation that she still has worth.'"

"Now who's the psychologist?" I muttered with a shake of my head. "Who was that? James? Melinda from the diner?"

I couldn't stop the nagging feeling that they were right. That I didn't belong here—that I was trying to make up for something. Even if I couldn't fix my own life, maybe I could fix someone else's.

"Why don't we talk inside, where there aren't so many eyes," Sheriff Potts said, glancing up the road. It could have been my imagination, but I swore her tone was a little softer, and she seemed almost...sympathetic. I didn't see anyone else out and about, but that didn't mean they weren't there, watching.

There was no way we could talk inside about what she had to say, though. Not with my kids there.

"Out here is fine."

Sheriff Potts hesitated. "I'm sorry I've started things off on such a sour note—it's a bad habit of mine. But it doesn't get any better. The reason I'm here is because I've just heard back from the county medical examiner. It's not looking good for those of you at the party. And I need to find out who isn't being completely truthful."

"You're saying that based on your findings, her death wasn't accidental. Or natural."

The sheriff's hard gaze giving way to uncertainty. "I don't know. All indicators point to Marci Bailey eating something she shouldn't have. She had a deadly allergic reaction. End of story. That's impossible, though. According to everyone who was there, dinner hadn't even been served. No one ate anything at the party. So how could she have had the allergic reaction that she did?"

I hadn't eaten anything, but the image of hungry party guests who were waiting on a still-cooking-roast came to mind. "That might not be completely accurate," I said, my words slow.

Sheriff Potts' hard gaze returned. "Meaning..."

"We didn't technically have dinner. But there may have been some antsy folks who were finding it hard to wait."

I hesitated, wondering if I should tell the sheriff that Mrs. Bailey had been one of the impatient ones. I really didn't want to get Debbie into more trouble than she already was, though—there was no way she was responsible for Mrs. Bailey's death. She'd been trying to impress the councilwoman, not harm her. Besides, the puff pastries had been filled with cream cheese—I'd heard Kandy say so.

As someone who'd once had all evidence pointing to me in a crime I didn't commit, I wasn't about to do the same thing to Debbie.

If the sheriff's gaze had been hard before, it was nothing compared to now. "I need a complete list of what was eaten, and who ate it. Every detail. If Marci Bailey was murdered, I'm going to find the proof I need. And don't think you're not still high on the list, Ms. Swallows. I'll be corroborating what you tell me with the others."

"Someone was murdered?" a voice rang out from the direction of the front door. Flash ran toward me, his eyes lit up in excitement.

I put on my happy mom face, the one I wore when I

didn't want the kids to worry, even if they had every reason to. "Hey, buddy. I'm just talking with the sheriff about a hypothetical situation. Why don't you go back inside, and then we'll go get that pizza I promised you."

Flash didn't buy it for a minute, and I supposed I hadn't expected him to. He was too smart for that. "No way. Someone was murdered. I heard the sheriff say so. That is so cool. What was the weapon? Do you think they'll strike again?"

My innards shriveled up, and I wanted to crawl into a hole so deep, no one would ever be able to find me. Least of all the sheriff. She raised an eyebrow.

"I know how that sounds," I said, "but due to their dad's line of work, the kids have been exposed to a lot of stuff that kids their age have no business being around." When the sheriff stayed quiet, I realized I was making it worse.

"Not that he himself...you know...does that to people or anything like that. Their dad's not involved with the mafia or something similarly ridiculous."

"Dad says the mafia don't count as serial killers, even though they kill a lot of people," Flash said, nodding solemnly.

I moved to physically take the boy inside, but Sheriff Potts gave me a look that froze me mid-step. This of course encouraged Flash because he now had an audience, and he excitedly continued.

"Serial killers do it for the enjoyment. Because they

have something messed up in their heads. But organized crime folks do it as a means of control. Can't have your people going rogue when you're involved in illegal business, you know."

A mixture of emotions flashed across Sheriff Potts' face. She seemed both stunned and impressed. But then there was concern, most likely for the type of environment my children had been raised in.

"What did you say your husband does for work?" the sheriff asked, her gaze finding me.

"Psychology professor. Studies the psyche of serial killers. I always hated it, but I suppose that's just one of many reasons he's now my ex-husband." The sheriff raised an eyebrow. "Murder isn't one of them." I hadn't thought I'd needed to clarify that, but in light of recent circumstances, I felt the inclination to do so. Just in case.

Sheriff Potts nodded, like she was thinking. "Swallows," she finally said, like something was clicking into place. "Your ex-husband wouldn't be Cameron Swallows, would it?"

"You've heard of him."

"Don't know anything about him, but my sister is obsessed with true-crime podcasts. The other day she was trying to tell me about this book of his. She'd already pre-ordered it and everything."

My lips turned down into a frown. "Of course she did." A curious expression passed the sheriff's face, and I followed up with, "Nothing against your sister, of course.

I've just never been into that kind of thing. Made it difficult to have a conversation when he always wanted to talk about his latest research, and I wanted nothing more than to plug my ears, hum, and walk away. The stuff he studies is what nightmares are made of."

"I see." Sheriff Potts made another note on her pad, then slipped it back into her pocket.

I desperately wished I could see what she'd written. Did she believe me? Had my words been enough for her to think me innocent? Had I said too much?

"If you need anything else, stop on by," I said. "I'm more than happy to help." My tone was chipper, my smile too wide. Rather than coming across like an innocent do-gooder as I'd intended, I had the feeling I resembled the Joker.

"For right now, the list of food that was eaten prior to my arrival will suffice."

As the sheriff turned to leave, Flash called, "Bye, Sheriff!" then ran toward the house, yelling, "Lilly, you'll never guess what happened. Someone was murdered and Mom's a suspect! I can't wait to tell Dad when he gets back."

_____

7

The next morning found me sitting at my kitchen table, pen in hand. I blew a strand of hair from my face as I tapped it against a blank piece of paper, attempting to recreate events from the night of the...incident.

"I really don't want to do this," I said to Trish. "If I write what I know, the sheriff is going to go after Debbie with everything she has, and we both know that Debbie didn't kill Mrs. Bailey." Trish was cleaning up after making homemade fudge, insisting that people who were being investigated for murder didn't need to watch their weight. I agreed.

I could at least tell the sheriff about the rolls that James Rodney ate, and the meat and cheese consumed by Kandy. While debating if I should mention Mrs. Bailey, I whacked the pen a little too hard against the table, and it went flying out of my hands and onto the floor. When I reached down to pick it up, a flash of gray knocked it away, sending it skittering across the kitchen floor.

"Ava." I groaned. Why didn't that cat pick on someone its own size? Or at least vary it once in a while. I stood, prepared to snatch my pen back from the cat, but another whack sent it flying into the living room. As much as I didn't want Ava to believe she'd gotten the upper hand, I was also not in the mood to go chasing her all over the house.

Trish laughed and pulled a pen out of the junk drawer. "No worries, I'll get it back from her later." She handed me the pen and went back to the dishes. "Really, you should be flattered. She doesn't pay attention to people unless she likes them. And considering how much attention you get from her..." She lifted a shoulder. "I'd say that you are her favorite."

"Sorry, Trish, but your logic is faulty." I sat back down at the table. "She snuggles with you, and she attacks me. Enough said."

I turned my attention back to the dinner party. "Both James and Mrs. Bailey peeked into a couple of pots on the stove, but they only smelled the contents. Is that enough to set off an allergic reaction? One of them was corn chowder. I didn't get a glimpse of the other."

"Pazole," Trish said. "Pretty sure it was pork and not human meat, though."

I slowly turned to face her. "I'm sorry, I think I missed

the part where we were going off the assumption that Debbie is both a murderer and a cannibal."

Trish grinned. "According to Cameron, in ancient times, pazole was made with the meat of prisoners and served to the community as part of a sacred ritual. You know, once they ripped..."

I held up a hand. "Okay, I get it. Apparently, everyone but me is fascinated with Cameron and his gruesome tales. You, the kids, the sheriff's sister—"

"When did you meet the sheriff's sister? I thought Potts wasn't from around here."

"She's not." I gave a quick shake of my head. "Can we get this over with so I can deliver this to the sheriff and be done with it? I wish she'd at least given me a hint as to what they'd discovered about Mrs. Bailey's death. It's the not knowing that's the worst of it. What was in the food that killed her?"

I stared at the paper in front of me, but instead of words, unwanted thoughts lambasted me. Thoughts that Sheriff Potts' visit had brought with it.

Thoughts of no one wanting me here. No one wanting my and Trish's business, even though they desperately needed it. No one giving me the benefit of the doubt.

A knock on the door startled me. Before the dinner party, I hadn't had a single visitor. Now, they wouldn't stay away. And they were the kind of visitors I could do without.

"Probably Sheriff Potts again," I grumbled as I moved

to open the door. But rather than the sheriff, Debbie stood on the front porch. And she was in tears.

Guilt accosted me. I should have checked on her after the party. Made sure she was okay.

"Debbie, come in," I said, ushering her inside. Were murder suspects allowed to hang out together? I didn't see why not. The sheriff had already taken all our statements, so it wasn't like we could change our stories now.

Debbie sniffled and walked inside, but then stopped short in the entryway. "I'm sorry. I shouldn't be here."

"Nonsense," Trish said, hurrying forward and handing Debbie a piece of fudge, like that had been why she'd been visiting in the first place. "Witnessing a death is traumatic, but for it to be in your own home... Well, that's something else entirely."

Debbie nodded, a stray tear escaping. "I'd been booked with back-to-back hair appointments this week. All but two have canceled. And I'm fairly certain those two just wanted to see the place where Mrs. Bailey died." She pulled in a shuddered breath.

I felt so bad for Debbie. She'd thrown the party in an attempt to expand her business and had instead lost all her clients. "Is there anything we can do?"

"I'm just sorry you all got mixed up in it," Debbie said miserably. She pinched off a piece of fudge and stuck it in her mouth. "I mean, honestly, Mrs. Bailey is dead, my guests and I have all been accused of murder, including the mayor—not something that will help him gain re-election when the time comes, I'm sure—and now I've just heard that Potts and her deputy are looking extra close at his girlfriend, Katie. Hard feelings have been brewing just under the surface for a while now, but I'm afraid Mrs. Bailey's death is what's going to make them boil over."

Anxiety gripped me, and my breath escaped in a whoosh. I slumped onto a couch, forcing my heart to slow.

I didn't know this town anymore. Or the people. Not enough to understand the dynamics at play. I couldn't be a part of this—didn't know what was expected of me. I'd had to clear my name once before. Nothing to do with murder, but the same sick feeling that I'd had then returned. Because maybe I didn't know my town anymore, but I hated to think that someone I had grown up with could be capable of something so horrendous. Or that they would think the same thing of me.

I didn't want to believe it was murder.

But even though the sheriff knew the people of this town less than I did, she seemed to be convinced it was. Which made her dangerous. Accusations could land anywhere, without any context.

A tiny voice told me that made her perfect for the job —someone who was objective. Didn't allow emotions to get in the way.

Unlike me, who was trying to protect Debbie, even though I had nothing but gut feelings to rely on.

"Do you have any idea who might have wanted to hurt Mrs. Bailey?" I asked Debbie, giving her a side glance as she moved to sit on the opposite end of the couch. "Anyone at all."

Debbie wiped at a tear as she released a humorless laugh. "Sure. How about the entire town?"

My surprise must have been evident, because Debbie laughed again, but this one sounded far more genuine.

"You've been gone for a long time, Maddie. Mrs. Bailey was intolerable when we were young, but unlike fine cheese or wine, she got worse as she aged. A bit senile too, if you ask me. Always accusing people of ridiculous things. Once she accused Al Cromby, you know, the owner of the market, of stealing cereal boxes out of her cupboard so he could resell them. And I think you were right when you said she's the reason James hasn't allowed me to rent space from him, even though it's sitting there empty, not making him a dime. Probably told him I use shampoo that makes my clients' hair fall out."

Trish appeared by my side with a glass of water, and I gave her an appreciative smile before turning back to Debbie. I could always count on Trish to have my back, whether I asked for it or not.

"James seems like the kind of man that could hold his own, though," I said. "Anything he's doing Mrs. Bailey may have influenced, but his actions are his own."

Debbie held up her hands, as if telling me not to shoot the messenger. "I know it doesn't make sense, but that woman has had James in her pocket for the last decade. I don't know what she has on him, but for years they've voted the same way for every issue that comes before the town council. Something's going on there, but no one has ever been able to figure out what."

Maybe not. But now that Mrs. Bailey was dead, it was about time James Rodney shared with the class. Because right now my hometown was being torn apart, my friends and I were being accused of the worst sorts of atrocities, and that was not the kind of town I had promised my family.

Not to mention, I really didn't want to go to jail for a murder I hadn't committed.

"Where do the Rodneys live?" I asked Debbie.

"Las Collinas. One street over from town hall. White house with blue shutters. You can't miss it."

Trish's lips dipped into a frown. "You aren't actually thinking of going over there, are you? He's probably the one who did it, you know."

"Sheriff Potts is doing her best, I'm sure. But all three of our necks are on the chopping block, and we need answers. Answers that don't involve jail time."

"It's been two days," Trish said.

I stood and grabbed my jacket off the back of the couch. "Yes, and that's two days that I've been going out of my mind with worry. She could at least tell us what Mrs. Bailey actually died from—what their findings were. She could tell me why I'm still high on her suspect list. I have kids, Trish. I've already had the experience of others thinking of me as less than honest—been a suspect in a crime I didn't commit. But a stolen cat urn wouldn't have landed me in prison for the rest of my life."

Trish gave a quick nod. "All right. But I'm coming with. You know, as backup."

I gave her a sad smile. She really was the best friend a woman could ask for. I didn't know of anyone else who would volunteer to come visit a potential murderer's house with me. But this was something I needed to do on my own.

"Sorry, but the Rodneys will be more likely to talk to me if I'm alone. If we all go, it might feel like we're ganging up on them."

"What if it were two teenagers?" Lilly called from the top of the staircase. She thundered down with Flash on her heels. She had her phone in hand, and I could see the camera app was pulled up, like she was ready to start filming. This wasn't an impromptu decision. I wondered how much those two knew—how often they'd been listening in when I hadn't realized. More than made me comfortable, for sure.

"No one ever pays attention to us. We're more of a nuisance," Flash said, grinning. "But we can help."

Trish threw me an amused smile, like she was wondering how I was going to talk my way out of this one.

The hard part was, I really did want to let them tag along. Lilly had barely looked at me since returning home the previous day, let alone since we'd moved to Amor, and she and Flash rarely got along. And yet here they were tag teaming.

Except, this wasn't a day out on the town, and this wasn't what I had meant when I'd said I wanted to spend more time as a family.

"I'm sorry," I said. I hoped they saw that I meant it. "But the answer is no for you two as well."

Lilly frowned, and I immediately wanted to do anything to make her smile return.

"I can film the entire interaction without them even knowing," she said. "Then we can replay it—look at their reactions after your questions. Analyze their expressions and body language. Flash and I can help. I know we can."

I had raised Lilly well, a girl after my own heart. Like me, she was a people watcher. And she'd heard enough of my and her dad's psychology babble to have learned a thing or two. The girl had a point. But it didn't matter how helpful they could be. I would never forgive myself if something happened to them.

My face must have said it all, because Lilly's eyes narrowed, and her grip on her phone tightened.

Without another word, she spun around and ran back upstairs, taking the steps two at a time. Flash followed closely, calling her name as he ran.

"Did I make a mistake?" I asked, turning toward Trish and Debbie.

Debbie shrugged, like there wasn't a good answer. But Trish had one for me.

"Oh yeah, sure. You won't let them watch TV past nine o'clock, for their own good, of course. But not taking them on a murder investigation—they're never going to forgive you for that one. You should feel ashamed of yourself." Trish's tone dripped with amused sarcasm, which I returned by sticking my tongue out at her. Like the mature adults that we were.

And then I left the house, not wanting to wait another minute. Because if I did, I knew I'd let Trish and Debbie talk me out of it. I shouldn't be going alone. I shouldn't be going at all. I knew that.

But right now, the sheriff believed there was a murderer in town. And I needed to stop the rumor mill from saying it was me, or my friends.

8

W hite house with blue shutters. Check. A black car sat in the driveway, but that didn't mean the Rodneys were home. I stared up at the house for long enough that if anyone in the nearby homes were watching me from their windows, they might suspect that James and Kandy were the next victims on my list.

James was ornery. And unfair. But was he really capable of murder?

Maybe. It was difficult to really know what anyone was capable of.

Including you, an unwanted voice said. Yes, I supposed me included.

But I knew I hadn't done it, and I didn't know where else to start but with the man who had apparently been controlled by Mrs. Bailey for who knew how many years.

A silver car rolled by, and my heart picked up, but the car continued on and around the corner.

I forced my breathing to slow. It wasn't like I was in any real danger. Just coming over to ask the Rodneys a few harmless questions. To be honest, who I really wanted to talk to was Kandy. Alone. Her tongue seemed to loosen whenever her husband wasn't around.

I never had the chance to knock—didn't even make it up the walkway—before the front door opened.

James stood there, arms folded across his chest. "You going to stand out there all day, staring, or was there something you wanted?"

Too late to change my mind now.

"I have a couple of questions," I said, hurrying forward. "About town council. Would you mind if I picked your brain for a few minutes?"

James Rodney's forehead furrowed until his eyebrows met in the middle. I couldn't tell if it was from annoyance or concentration. "All right."

This was it. I was entering the infamous James Rodney's home. I had been terrified of him as a child, and he wasn't any less terrifying now. But I plastered on a smile and followed him inside. I desperately hoped that Kandy was home.

"You planning on running for town council?" James asked, his tone gruff. "Now that Marci is gone, there is a spot available, I suppose. From the sounds of it, you'll have a tough go of it. Lots of competition. Hasn't been an available spot in six years. Those of us on the council never lose when it's time for re-election, you know. The town knows we do what needs to be done to preserve our town."

"Does anyone even bother running against you anymore?"

His lips twitched up into a smile. "No. I suppose that makes the re-election more of a formality, doesn't it?"

"Except when you ran for mayor. Probably thought you had it in the bag."

James's smile dipped. "The folks in Amor struggle with change. Keeping a Freedman in office was comforting for them. But they see now what a mistake that was."

He motioned for me to follow him down a set of stairs to a den, where it looked like James had been reading before I'd interrupted him, a book splayed out on the couch.

"To answer your question, no, I don't plan on running." I sat down on the edge of the couch, careful not to disturb the book. *Cooking as a Passion: A Guide to Unlocking Culinary Perfection.* "I don't think I'd ever be able to fill Mrs. Bailey's shoes—wouldn't even try."

"Good. That means I won't have to try to let you down easy. Folks would never vote you in. CJ down at the auto repair shop has a better chance at town council than you, considering your...situation."

"I don't know that my situation is any different from yours," I said. "We're both suspects in a murder investigation. I suppose that might affect your own re-election. If someone bothered to run against you."

The moment the words left my lips, I wished I could take them back.

James's gaze hardened. "The town knows I didn't do it. Marci and I were friends. Always looking out for the good of our neighbors. I would never do anything to harm her, or this town."

Friends. I doubted that.

"I'm sorry. I didn't mean to insinuate otherwise. I know you love this town, and you've given so much to it."

"Why are you really here?"

From the look on James's face, I didn't have long before he kicked me out. "It wasn't to throw around accusations, I assure you. I am genuinely curious," I said, choosing my words carefully. "How does town council work? I've been gone so long, and I would truly like to understand how local government works. I'd like to be involved. For example, what happens if you disagree with your fellow council members? Does a vote need to be unanimous? Does the mayor have the final say?"

I watched James Rodney closely. His gaze seemed slightly less terrifying than it had a second earlier, and he sat down in a reclining chair across from me. Silence settled over us, and he seemed to be calculating his next response. I shifted uncomfortably on the couch.

"There are seven members on town council, and as long as four of us vote in favor of an issue, it passes. The mayor only votes if there is a tie, but with seven being an odd number, it's impossible for that to occur. He doesn't have as much power over the town as one would think."

"Huh." I tried to look only mildly interested, as though a thought hadn't just occurred to me that had started the gears turning. As it stood, there was now an even number of council members. It seemed the mayor had a lot more power today than he'd had two days ago.

James eyed me warily, and I made sure my smile was securely in place. "Is that it? After hiding out in that dilapidated house of yours for nearly two months, you dropped by unannounced to ask me about town council?"

I tried to look embarrassed. "I'm sorry. You're right. I wasn't completely truthful. I heard of Debbie's situation with her business, the poor woman, and came to ask you to reconsider your decision. She is in desperate need of a real salon, and I believe the town would be better for it."

James snorted. "Poor woman, indeed. It's not that I don't want to rent the space to Debbie—heaven knows Kandy and I could use the extra money. Working as a writer for the *Amor Gazette* doesn't exactly pay in monetary rewards. But do you have any idea the kinds of chemicals that are used in a hair salon? Ammonia, sodium hydroxide, not to mention phenylenediamine.

"Do you realize how toxic they are? When breathed in, they can do damage to your liver, kidneys...even your nervous system. And I'm going to send folks into that kind of environment? Those chemicals will stay in the walls and be nearly impossible to get out. When we were at Debbie's party, you must have noticed the smell. I was getting dizzy just being there and was certain we'd all be violently ill by the end of the evening. I bet that was the real culprit behind Marci's death. Those chemicals. No, I'm sorry, I can't do anything about what Debbie does in her own home. But I can stop her from spreading her poison in my rental space."

He glanced at his watch. "You'll have to excuse me. I'm working on a deadline."

My gaze followed his and landed on a side room off the den. The door was partially open, and I could see a computer and stacks of paper around it. "Sure, I understand. I'm sorry I took you away from your work. I did have just one more question before I leave."

"Yes?"

"Did you notice if anyone managed to eat at the party? Never mind the countdown to the new year, I was awake until midnight just trying to find something to satisfy my hunger." I gave what I hoped was a casual laugh.

James stared at me for a moment. "Careful, Maddie. You're starting to sound like the sheriff. And she's not particularly liked around here."

Okay, maybe I wasn't as stealthy as I liked to give myself credit for. "Yes, I suppose I do." My gaze dropped and I tried to look repentant. "What I really want to know is if anyone ate the same thing that Mrs. Bailey did."

"You want to know if she was poisoned. And if any of

us ate the same thing she did, we would have gotten sick too."

Based on Sheriff Potts' visit the previous day, I was fairly certain it hadn't been poison, but James didn't need to know that. "Just covering all my bases."

"They aren't your bases to cover."

Right he was.

"Thank you for your time, Mr. Rodney."

James nodded, then stood from his recliner. I mirrored the action and turned to leave.

"Oh, and Maddie?" he said.

I paused, glancing back at him.

"Be careful where you're snooping. I'm a newspaper man and can tell you there's a fine line between curiosity and meddling. And as it turns out, it doesn't matter which it is. Both can be equally dangerous."

My heart constricted. Was that a warning? A threat?

"Thank you. I'll keep that in mind," I said, then saw myself out. Because the air in the room had suddenly gone cold.

Once outside, I sucked in a lungful of air. I was out of my element here. What had I been thinking, going over there?

I already knew the answer to that. I wanted to clear my name. I wanted reassurance that I had done the right thing, dragging my kids away from their friends and schools. That this was a good place to raise my family.

A lot of good it had done. I hadn't even gotten the

chance to ask about James's relationship with Mrs. Bailey but was certain he would have thrown me out the second I had.

Music burst from my phone, startling me. I pulled it out of my pocket and glanced at the screen. It was a number I didn't recognize. Probably a scammer. I let the call go to voicemail. It started ringing again.

Scammers had apparently gotten more persistent, and I answered the call to tell them as much. But I didn't get further than "Whatever is it you're—"

"Maddie, I stopped by your place to see how the faucet was treating you." Benji. The sound of his voice brought back memories of bonfires in the desert and the smell of roasting sausages. Green chile. My lips tilted up into a small smile. Except, as he continued, I noted a tone of urgency. Panic. "Trish said you'd gone to James's place. I wanted to warn you that—"

"Ms. Swallows, interesting place to find you."

I turned slowly and found myself facing Sheriff Potts.

"Hey, Mom, I'm going to have to call you back." I ended the call and slipped the phone back into my pocket. "Just going for an afternoon stroll. Got to get those endorphins going, you know. Fresh air. All the good stuff."

Sheriff Potts' lips dipped into a frown. "Ms. Swallows, I don't like it when people lie to me. Makes me think they're up to something."

I didn't answer.

"Imagine my surprise to find Debbie at your home when I stopped by for a little chat."

Another one? The sheriff must not have been joking when she'd said I was high on her list of suspects.

I folded my arms over my chest to keep my hands from giving away how nervous the sheriff made me. "Yes. The woman is distraught, as you can imagine. We're friends. Friends comfort each other. That's what we do."

"So, you knew she was there. Which means you were there when she arrived."

The sheriff hadn't known that bit of information—she was fishing. Why?

"Like I said, nothing wrong with having a friend over."

"Yes, but three suspects in one place, and then I find out you are on your way to visit another two. You seem to be covering your bases quite thoroughly."

"Two?"

Sheriff Potts nodded toward the house behind me. "James and Kandy?"

"Oh, right." I released a nervous chuckle. James's voice entered my thoughts, telling me that these weren't my bases to cover. That it was the sheriff's job. "That was nothing. Just me asking James some technical questions about town council."

"Is that why you were secretly filming him through his window? That seems like a bit more than nothing."

My jaw went slack. "W-what? I really have no idea what

you're talking about. I would never do something like that."

"Maybe you wouldn't, but your children didn't seem to have any qualms about it."

My heart felt like it had slid into my stomach. Yes, my children would do something like that. Follow me, even after I had asked them not to. Sneak into someone's backyard. Sheriff Potts' deputy was just rounding the corner of the house, my teenagers walking behind him, their gazes on the ground.

They were good actors, I'd give them that.

But I caught the quick smile that Lilly threw Flash. The one that said they knew something the deputy didn't. The one that said they didn't mind getting caught, because they had gotten what they needed.

But I didn't see how they could have. James had had his back to the window the entire time. It had been me who had been facing the window.

Unless something about my expression while we'd been talking had said more than I'd meant it to.

"Would you two like to explain one more time why you were hiding in the Rodneys' backyard?" the sheriff said, giving them a pointed look.

"We thought you were sneaking out to meet a man," Lilly said, her gaze remaining on her shoes. "And we were right."

Flash gave a slow nod and pretended to cry. "I don't

want a new dad. Please. Especially not Mr. Rodney. I'll run away, I swear I will."

I gave Flash a look of warning and hoped he understood what it meant. That this wasn't a daytime soap opera and he needed to dial the drama down a notch, or the sheriff wouldn't believe a word of it.

"We'll talk about this at home." My tone was brisk, and I nodded down the street. "Come on, let's go. As we walk, you can think about what punishment might be appropriate for the situation."

Flash wailed. "We even have to choose our own punishment? How cruel can you be, Mother? It isn't fair. It isn't!"

Even he must have realized he'd gone a bit far, because he threw a quick glance at the sheriff, whose eyebrows had risen. His gaze dropped to his shoes. Lilly had yet to look at me, but I was fairly certain it was because she was on the brink of laughter.

As I turned to lead my children home, the sheriff said, "Oh, Lilly?"

My daughter stilled. "Yes?"

"May I see that phone?"

I was tempted to panic, but Lilly handed it over without hesitation.

As the sheriff flipped through the pictures, time seemed to slow, and I braced myself for the worst. After what felt like an eternity, she handed it back to Lilly. "If something interesting were to show up on that phone, I'd expect you to tell me."

Lilly nodded.

Once we were out of earshot, she whispered, "Wait until you see what we got.

9

I waited until we were home to comment on anything but the weather. Sheriff Potts seemed to show up everywhere. But as soon as we were inside, I turned on Lilly.

"What were you two thinking, following me like that? Recording people within their homes. That's illegal, by the way. And dangerous."

Lilly's expression slackened. "You're mad? First you don't like that I'm holed up in my room—you want me to get out more—and now you're telling me I should have stayed home?"

"Lilly, I wanted you to make some friends. Not take your brother out to secretly record me through a murder suspect's window."

Flash jumped between us. "Mom, let her talk. We've been hearing all sorts of crazy things. Your conversations with Trish, for one thing." His gaze dropped. "We wanted to help."

"I noticed something when I was looking back at my video diary from a few days ago," Lilly said. "In the background. I thought it might be useful."

They both looked at me expectantly. What was I supposed to say? My two teenagers knew there had been a murder at the party that Trish and I attended. They knew that the sheriff hadn't ruled me out as a suspect. And I'd always taught them to use their talents to help others.

Lilly was actually showing interest in something other than wandering around town with her phone, recording her tragic upbringing for whatever future progeny happened to stumble upon her video diary. I was certain ninety percent of that diary was complaining about what a horrible mother she had to deal with.

But a potential murder investigation—this was something that children shouldn't be a part of.

At the same time, if Lilly had recorded something that would help us figure out who the killer was, it would be irresponsible of me not to watch it. More people could get hurt.

"All right. What do you have?"

Lilly's expression lit up. "Really? You mean it?"

In spite of the anxiety that made me feel like I had swallowed an anvil, I laughed. "Sure. Let's see what you have on that thing."

It didn't take more than thirty seconds for her to fly up the stairs and return with her computer in hand.

"I automatically sync my videos to the cloud," Lilly said, setting it up on the kitchen table. Her fingers flew across the keys as she entered her password and pulled something up. "This afternoon at the Rodneys' house, I deleted the video from my phone before showing it to the sheriff, but it had already uploaded." She clicked on an icon, and a video popped up.

Lilly made sure the volume was off and then clicked play. She fast-forwarded about ten minutes into the video.

I recognized the street she was walking along. It was Debbie's street.

"Can you turn up the volume?" I asked.

Lilly gave me a look that said, *You're kidding, right?* "This is my diary, Mom. And we'd just had a fight. Trust me, you don't want to hear it."

She was probably right. This was the day her dad had picked her up for her New Year's Eve party, and I'd made Lilly change clothes after she'd modified a dress to be too short for my liking.

"Besides, it isn't me that makes the video interesting. Pay attention as I walk past Debbie's house."

I was about to ask how Lilly knew where Debbie lived, but then the hair stylist's house came into view, and Debbie walked out onto her front porch as if looking for someone.

A silver car pulled up in front of the house, and Debbie

smiled and waved. Lilly had nearly passed the house, but in the far corner of the screen, I saw someone get out of the passenger side of the car. Kandy. It was only a couple of blocks from her own house, so why had she bothered to get a ride?

"What time was this at?" I asked Lilly, reaching over to pause it.

She checked the upload time. "Eleven a.m."

I stared at the screen, trying to make sense of it. "Seven hours before the party was meant to start. And she is having someone drop her off. Or maybe visiting Debbie with a second person who didn't want to bother walking?" I squinted. Kandy was holding something. Something wide. Maybe a tray?

"Who did she drive over with?" Trish asked, leaning over my shoulder. "James?"

The image was cut off, and I could only see the edge of the driver's seat, not who was in it.

"Maybe. But that isn't his car. The one that was parked in their driveway was black, not silver."

"There's more," Lilly said, excitement tinging her voice, like she was trying not to let me know how much she was enjoying playing sleuth. "The video I erased earlier." She exited out of the current video and pulled up a new one.

This wasn't a video of James and me talking in his den. Lilly had begun filming as she'd approached the house. She seemed to be hiding behind a parked car with Flash, and I saw myself on the sidewalk in front of the Rodneys' house.

Lilly paused the video as James opened the door and invited me in.

"Look to the left of the house," she said, then un-paused it.

There was Kandy, and she was coming around the back and through the gate. With a backward glance at the house, she hurried down the street and out of the video frame.

"What are you doing?" I murmured as she disappeared. Why had she felt like she had to sneak away?

The cooking book on the couch. It had been hers.

"Maybe I spoke with the wrong Rodney."

"Or maybe you just didn't ask the right questions," Trish said.

That was more like it. I hadn't been treating people as patients but as clues to a crime. How many times in a therapy session had things been uncovered that not only surprised me but surprised my patient as well? Things they had forgotten or hadn't realized were important.

Or things they hadn't wanted anyone to know but got comfortable enough talking to me that they let it slip.

No one was going to open up to the sheriff. The woman was formidable, not to mention new to town. A stranger. No one trusted her. No one would truly be honest, even if they weren't the guilty party.

Which meant that if we were going to put an end to this, I needed to put on my psychologist hat.

"Okay, folks. We need to make a list of all the suspects, including myself, and write down what we know."

"Before you do," Flash said, "I have my own clue to share. It's not a video, but I think it's just as good." He ran upstairs, and I shared an anxious look with Trish. Not a minute later, Flash was already back downstairs and opening his laptop. "The medical records in this place have no protection except a silly password. Seriously, it's like they are holding the door open for anyone to walk through."

I had been right to be nervous. My heart stuttered. "You broke into the local medical records? You promised me that with all the computer stuff you do, hacking is not one of them. That you don't do anything illegal."

"I don't usually, but this is important," Flash protested. "And it wasn't Amor's medical records that I looked into."

I supposed that was a small relief.

"It was the state's."

And the panic was back.

It must have been obvious because Flash shot me a look of annoyance. "I don't know about you, but I'd rather if my mother wasn't a jailbird. Kids get bullied for stuff like that, you know. Not to mention that you wouldn't last more than a few hours in the type of place you'd be going. Dad told me all about it."

Yes, as a scare tactic to keep Flash on the straight and narrow. Not for situations like...this.

"And how do you think it's going to look, Flash, when they find out that the son of a murder suspect broke into the victim's medical records? It is not going to help my case, I promise."

"Mom, relax. They aren't going to find out. I make sure to not leave a trail." He started closing his laptop. "I guess if you don't want to know what I found out, I can just take this back upstairs. Keep the information to myself. No worries. I understand."

Oh, that boy was good. He knew I wanted to know what he'd found out. Besides, he'd already broken in, and I didn't want it to be for nothing.

"Fine. Tell us." I released an exasperated sigh. "But you are still in big trouble, mister. Grounded from your computer for a week."

Flash paled. "For trying to help you?" He yelped. "What about Lilly? She was filming Kandy and Debbie without them knowing. Isn't that illegal?"

I had no idea. Maybe. Probably not?

When I threw a look at Trish, she merely shrugged.

"Just tell us what you know, Flash."

He stared at me for a few beats, as if trying to decide if he wanted to tell me after all. "Fine," he finally said. "But don't think I'm ever going to break the law for you again. Not even if you beg." Flash threw in a glare for good measure, and then opened his computer back up.

"Because of the nature of the death, they'd immediately ordered a toxicology report as well as sent a sample of Mrs. Bailey's stomach contents to the lab. But it turns out there was no need. Plants have a cell wall that makes it so they digest more slowly than something like meat or cheese, which just turns to goop as soon as it hits the stomach acid."

"I'm assuming they didn't find any poison in her system," I said, remembering how the sheriff had said that the powers-that-be thought it was a case of accidentally ingesting something that Mrs. Bailey was allergic to.

Flash scrolled through the file, as if looking for something. "No poison. Looks like there was only one item that was able to be identified from the stomach. To be honest, I don't understand most of this. I just skim until I see something I recognize. But it does say that the stomach was nearly empty."

"Makes sense. We were all hungry, and she'd probably not eaten for several hours," I said. "But I already know what she ate. It was one of those puff pastries."

"You had puff pastries?" Flash groaned. "I knew I should have stayed home and gone to that party with you. I mean, I know Dad tried, but there are some things you just can't get at your local McDonald's, you know?"

"Honey, the puff pastries could have been what killed Mrs. Bailey. They could have been the murder weapon."

He shook his head. "Only if you were allergic to whatever was in them. According to our stupidly easily accessible report here, they had green chiles in them, if that's helpful at all to you."

I turned to Trish. "Are green chiles considered nightshades?"

"One internet search, coming right up," she said.

But by the time she'd pulled out her phone to check, Flash already had the answer. No one could compete with his quick-draw computer skills. "Yup, they are."

"Did Debbie know that?"

I couldn't help but take note that of all the food that was meant to be served, the green chile had resided in the one dish whose filling was hidden.

"I can call to find out," Trish said.

"No, that's all right. I'll go pay her a visit. Do you know where she went after she left here?"

"I assume she returned home, but I have no idea."

I didn't like this new role I'd thrust myself into. The one who felt the need to question my friends, to accuse them of things I could barely say out loud.

But I couldn't help but wonder if Debbie's visit to our home earlier had been more than just a visit from a distraught friend.

10

"Hey, I was just coming by to see you." Benji was walking up the walkway just as I left the house. "Thought I'd check on things between jobs. You cut me off last time we talked."

My mind was running at a million miles an hour, and I had to rein it in enough to be able to focus on Benji. "Hmm? Oh, yeah. The faucet. It's great."

"I'm not here about the faucet." He changed direction to walk with me, his pace matching mine. "You seem distracted. Everything okay?"

I raised an eyebrow, and his lips quirked up at the corners.

"You're right," he said. "Stupid question with everything going on." Benji's smile faded. "Look, you need to stay away from the Rodneys."

Benji now had my full attention. "What did you find out?"

"Only what it was that Marci had on James. The thing that was keeping him under her control." He straightened and gave me a smile that meant he was waiting for praise for a job well done.

"That's amazing. What did you find out?"

"Well," Benji said, lowering his voice to a conspiratorial whisper, "I was talking to Zoe, the mayor's assistant, as I was cleaning out her gutters. Apparently, Sam's dad, the former mayor, let it slip once that he'd always been suspicious about the first election that James had won to get onto town council. Nowadays it's all done electronically, but it wasn't that way back then. The mayor could never prove it, though, and it seems that the elections since then have been on the up and up. But if anyone could ever prove that first one was rigged, James would lose his position on town council, and any chance of what he's really after."

"He wants to be mayor," I said, remembering how relieved people had been that Sam had run against James in the previous mayoral election.

"Ding, ding, ding."

"You're saying that Mrs. Bailey had the proof to bring him down but instead used it to her advantage? Getting him to vote any way she needed?"

Benji nodded. "Zoe said she remembered a particular town council meeting, just before an important vote, where she'd heard Mrs. Bailey make what sounded like an offhand remark to James about rigged elections. Everyone else, including Zoe, had taken it as the usual paranoia that Mrs. Bailey was known for. But not James. He stormed from the room and didn't return. Mrs. Bailey didn't seem concerned, though—just smirked, and the meeting proceeded without him."

That was a really strong motive for murder. Having someone control you like that for so many years—it could make good people do bad things, not to mention bad people do even worse things.

Paying another visit to James didn't seem like the way to go, though. I doubted he'd give me anything new, and quite honestly, he would probably call Sheriff Potts on me for harassment. That was the last thing I needed.

And Debbie had just as strong a motive. Even if she didn't realize James Rodney's actual reasons for not wanting to rent to her, she still thought Mrs. Bailey was behind it. And Debbie certainly had the means, slipping that green chile into the puff pastries.

My breaths turned shallow as I realized I was in way over my head. Solving a murder wasn't nearly as simple as getting someone to talk about their feelings. Because once the skeletons started coming out of the closets, there was no way to push them back in, and now everyone seemed guilty.

Debbie. James. Even the mayor had motive.

"What do you know of Sam's girlfriend?" I asked.

From what I had gathered, she wasn't exactly a saint, though I didn't know much more than that. Would she do something like this if she thought it would help Sam?

"Katie?" A wariness that I'd never seen before crossed Benji's face. "I know what people are saying about her, and it's true that she's had a rough past. Not murder, though. Theft, for the most part. Whatever she had to do to survive. She arrived in town last year when her car broke down and Sam helped her out. Of course, we didn't know anything about her then. It all culminated when a dirty cop she'd worked for in Denver tracked her down here and hauled her away. Sheriff Potts and her deputy didn't bother to help—something about red tape. But Sam didn't care. He went after her. It was all very public, and neither the mayor nor Katie were portrayed in the best light."

I remembered my mom telling me about it, but I had thought she'd been exaggerating with the details. And I hadn't realized the woman still lived here.

"You think her less likely to do something like this than the Rodneys?"

Benji hesitated. "She cares about people—people the town would rather forget. There's an entire homeless population here that will sing praises to her name. Katie managed to get them all jobs, right under James Rodney's nose. He had no idea that our holiday festival last year was completely run by the homeless until it was too late to stop what Katie had started. He was furious."

Sounded like Katie cared about those that couldn't

stand up for themselves. Specifically, who couldn't stand up to people like Mrs. Bailey and the Rodneys. Did she think of herself as some kind of savior? Was that the type of person she was—doing bad things for the better good?

Benji ran a hand through his hair. "Look, from what I've heard, Sheriff Potts hasn't let Katie make a move without her knowing about it. When she's not keeping an eye on you and Debbie, that's where she is."

"And you don't think Katie did it," I guessed.

"I know people. I see how they live—no one tidies up for the handyman. They let all their secrets hang out. Like when a single bachelor suddenly has fewer empty pizza boxes and more throw pillows on the couch, I know that the bachelor isn't as single as he claims to be. Or someone who always had ice cream containers in the trash but now has baskets filled with fresh fruit. They're now watching their diet, for whatever reason."

"But someone with murderous intentions doesn't just leave a gun out with a note that says 'I did it,'" I said.

"You're right." Benji glanced around, as if taking in our surroundings for the first time. "Where are we headed?"

"I was headed to Debbie's house, but now I'm not so sure."

He nodded, but he seemed distracted. Like there was something else on his mind.

"Out with it," I said with a small smile.

"Why didn't you tell me you were back in town?" he asked, glancing at me. "You were my best friend, and then

POOF, you were gone. I only knew what you were up to because your mom would tell me in passing at the market or wherever I happened to see her. And when you returned a few weeks back, I heard rumors, but that was all they were. Rumors. Not the real thing."

As I searched for an answer, I realized I'd subconsciously folded my arms—a sign that I was closing myself off from him. Protecting myself. I unfolded them.

"When I left," I said slowly, "I was doing it to escape. Not escaping you, but this town. And when I came back, I could sense all the told-you-sos. I didn't want you to be one of them—couldn't bear to remember you as anything but Benji, my best friend. I didn't want to see you and then realize you were Benji, the stranger."

Benji surprised me by laughing. "After all we've been through? Not a chance. I still have a scar, by the way, from when you shot me in the leg with that nail gun."

I threw my arms up in the air. "It was an accident!"

"Accident or no, every time I see that scar, I think of you. You may have run away to the big city, but a part of you stayed here in Amor. Maybe that was what dragged you back, even if it was kicking and screaming."

I snorted. "No, what dragged me back was a stupid cat urn."

Benji gave me a blank look. "You lost me."

"Another story for another day. Suffice it to say that the theft of a cat urn set off a series of unfortunate events that ultimately led me here. My kids hate me for it, as does my ex-husband. But I couldn't stay there anymore. I had to—"

"Run." Benji finished the sentence for me. "You've always been a runner."

I huffed. "Leaving unpleasant circumstances doesn't mean I'm running from my problems. Besides, despite what people's opinions of me are around here, I'm not running from Amor this time. I'm back, and opening up my own business, no less."

"You've been here less than two months and you've already considered leaving. Admit it."

So what if I had? I hadn't followed through with it. I was still here, determined to make it work and give it a real shot. If nothing else, for the kids.

Even with a murder hanging over our heads.

"Benji, I'm sorry I didn't call. Or write. Or keep in touch. I really am and have no good excuse. Let me make it up to you. Have any good restaurants opened up while I've been gone? I'll buy you dinner, and we can catch up."

His smile returned, reminding me of the Benji I'd once known. "How about you take me out once all this murder business is over with. As a celebration. But we don't need a fancy new restaurant to do it right."

"You don't mean..."

"Absolutely. It's still around, as ghostly as ever."

We had reached the end of the sidewalk, and I turned left onto Debbie's street, while Benji turned right. "I didn't like that place twenty years ago. What makes you think I want to go now?" I called after him.

"Because you secretly loved it, in spite of all your claims. And because it's exactly what you need to feel like you've come home. Bring the kids. They'll love it."

Yes, they probably would love a good old-fashioned ghost town nestled in the middle of the desert. Maybe Benji was right. Maybe that was just what we needed.

"All right, you got yourself a deal. But business first, then pleasure."

Benji laughed and waved at me over his shoulder as he headed to wherever he'd parked his truck with all his handyman supplies.

Business. I guessed that was how I was referring to murder investigations nowadays. But it really was business, in my case. If this murder went unsolved, there would always be a finger pointed in my direction, and Trish and I could kiss our own business aspirations goodbye.

SHERIFF POTTS WAS at Debbie's house when I arrived. Thank goodness her squad car gave her away, or I'd be in even worse trouble with the sheriff than I already was. I decided to walk around the block a couple of times while I waited for them to finish up and work toward my ten thousand steps for the day. Not that I generally tried hard to get them in. I usually didn't even get five thousand, let alone ten. But it made me feel less stalkerish going for a walk than hiding until the sheriff decided to leave.

I ended up making it five laps around the block before the sheriff got tired of interrogating Debbie. Maybe I was wrong. Maybe the sheriff actually knew how to do her job, and more efficiently than I could ever hope to.

But when Debbie answered the door, instead of finding my friend in tears as she had been the previous day, she looked fierce. Angry.

"I suppose you think I murdered Mrs. Bailey too, right?" she asked the moment she'd pulled open the door. Her lips were in a tight angry line, daring me to say otherwise.

I shook my head, as if questioning Debbie had been the furthest thing from my mind. As if I didn't know that green chile had somehow made it into the puff pastries.

"The sheriff has no good reason for harassing you as she has," I said, knowing full well that wasn't true.

It seemed Debbie knew it too, because the tears returned. "Yes, she does. It was my fault Mrs. Bailey died. I didn't know there was green chile. I swear I didn't. And I was so careful. But that doesn't matter much when someone is dead, does it?"

She opened the door wider and gestured for me to come in.

I noticed Debbie's pink bob was half curly, half straight today—like she'd slept on it wet and not bothered to fix it.

That wasn't at all like the hairstylist I knew, and suspicion was immediately replaced by concern.

"The sheriff isn't going to arrest you for the murder, is she?" I followed Debbie into the living room. Her house still smelled of hair chemicals. Even if she managed to open up her own salon, I doubted the smell would ever go away.

Debbie wiped at her eyes, smearing mascara down her cheeks. "I was shocked she didn't. But, even though I sound as guilty as they come, she didn't seem convinced. Like something was bothering her."

Relief swept over me. Against my better judgment, I was starting to warm up to the sheriff. Maybe even respect her a little. At least she wasn't the type to jump the gun and act first, ask questions later. That was more my ex-husband's style.

"You prepared all the food by yourself, though. How could green chile get into the food without you knowing?" I felt bad for baiting her, the image of Kandy arriving early in the day playing on repeat in my mind. Even if my friend wasn't guilty, I needed answers.

For the first time, I saw panic. Maybe some indecision? Like Debbie knew something she wasn't supposed to say.

"That was an awful lot of food to make by yourself," I continued. "If it had been me, I'd have taken any help I could get."

Debbie hesitated. "James Rodney is very particular about his food," she said slowly. "The food I made—they weren't my recipes. They were Kandy's. I told her how important this dinner was to me—she knows how difficult her husband can be. Kandy said that one time she spent three hours cooking a special meal for their anniversary, and James wouldn't even try it. Something about it being the wrong texture, like he could tell just by looking at it.

"I knew then that my plan of winning James over with a dinner party was the wrong way to go about it, but I had already invited everyone, so Kandy said she would help me out."

"She came over with her recipes and showed you how to make them." Thank goodness. I knew there had to be a perfectly good explanation. Except, if Debbie was innocent, that now meant Kandy was guilty. She'd been the only other one with access to the food.

Debbie nodded. "I'm a decent cook, but I'm not going to win any awards or anything. With only myself to cook for, I'm used to making small portions so I don't have too much left over. Cooking for nine people? I was in over my head."

"Kandy must not have shared her husband's same opinions about you renting from them."

The corner of Debbie's lips quirked up. "Oh, no. James doesn't know it, but she's one of my most loyal customers. I think she wants me in my own space nearly as badly as I do. It's not the most comfortable thing getting your hair washed over a kitchen sink, you know."

"And Kandy couldn't convince her husband?"

"No." Debbie's lips turned back down. "She tried. James wouldn't listen, though. Something about thinking I'm going to poison the town with my hair chemicals or whatever nonsense Mrs. Bailey was feeding him. He'd be furious if he ever found out that Kandy comes here as often as she does, let alone that she helped me cook for the party. I'd hoped that inviting people of influence would help him see reason, even if his wife couldn't."

"People like the mayor."

She nodded. "And town council. Mrs. Bailey could have turned James right around, if I'd had the chance to speak to her about it. Before...you know..." Debbie looked like she'd thought she'd said too much, her lips clamping shut and her gaze dropping. I knew I needed to switch into therapy mode if I was going to keep her talking.

"Did you tell the sheriff any of this?" I asked, my voice soft. "It could help convince her of your innocence. You weren't the only one cooking for the party, after all."

"Oh, no," Debbie said, her eyes widening. "I couldn't do that. Do you realize what James would do if he found out that Kandy was over here helping me? We cooked together the entire time and I didn't see even a hint of green chiles. No, telling the sheriff would create more problems than the alternative."

I nodded, like I understood, even though I didn't at all. Debbie needed to tell the sheriff what she knew, or she could be wrongfully convicted of a crime she didn't commit. Kandy's homelife must have been awful if Debbie was willing to stay silent in order to protect her.

"I'm sure the past couple of days have been hard on you. How are you holding up?"

Debbie's guard lowered further. "As well as you could expect. I feel guilty, you know."

"For Mrs. Bailey's death?"

"That, and the fact that you are all involved. I especially feel bad about Sam and Katie. The mayor is always under scrutiny as is and dating Katie hasn't made things any easier for him."

So Benji had implied.

"Why do you think Sam chose to date her? He must have known what the town would think of it. He's romantically involved with someone who has a questionable past, and they must wonder what kind of influence she has over him," I said, not yet having ruled Katie out as someone who could benefit from Mrs. Bailey's sudden demise, though I didn't see how she would have been able to pull it off.

Debbie was quiet for a moment, her gaze lifting to the ceiling as she thought. "I think," she finally said, her gaze returning to me, "that it's easy to look beyond someone's past when you're in love. And how that past might influence them. We want to be benevolent and give everyone a second chance. The mayor is a good guy that way. But when that past catches up with you the way it did with Katie—that crooked cop showing up and hauling her away

—I mean if it weren't for Sam, she'd probably be dead. Or at least back on the streets, lying and cheating people out of their money. Katie felt like she had to do everything that cop asked her to or else suffer the consequences. He had a lot of dirt on her. I get it. But it's difficult to escape a past like that. I'm not sure Sam fully realizes what he's gotten himself into, even now."

Sam had always had a level head and been more mature than the rest of us. Hard worker. I'd be lying if I said I wasn't surprised he'd even considered someone like Katie.

"Was there bad blood between Katie and Mrs. Bailey?" I asked.

Debbie stood, an indicator that she was tired of talking and was ready for me to leave. "I'm not sure if Katie knew Mrs. Bailey well enough for there to be bad blood."

Maybe. But I could confirm that it didn't take more than a minute in Mrs. Bailey's presence to have sudden murderous feelings.

11

I shouldn't have lied to Debbie, telling her I was hoping to get some of Kandy's recipes from the party. But I needed Kandy's phone number. No more randomly dropping in on the Rodneys' home. I'd forgotten that Debbie now had those same recipes and she'd offered to copy them down for me, so I had to follow it up with another lie about wanting to ask Kandy about specific cooking techniques.

It wasn't a complete fabrication, though. When I'd worked for the university, I hadn't had time to cook most evenings, and my family had become very familiar with the local restaurants and which ones had takeout. Since quitting my position there, we'd rarely eaten out, and I'd loved eating homecooked meals again. But I tended to get in a rut. I'd find something I liked and cook it over and over until the kids started complaining. A few new recipes would be a good thing.

When I finally managed to leave Debbie's and give Kandy a call, she answered but said she was at her sister's house. A visit would have to wait.

It was just as well. I knew that Kandy had had the opportunity to hurt Mrs. Bailey, but from my limited interactions with her, I didn't want to believe she would. Honestly, I liked her. If not Kandy, though, who?

My phone burst into song, and I saw it was Trish.

Shoot. I was supposed to meet her at our therapy office to help paint and choose a desk and chair from an office supply catalog.

I braced myself for a rebuke and answered. "Hey, Trish." My tone was too chipper and upbeat. I knew it the moment those two words slipped out.

"Hey, yourself. I know you know you're late, so save the 'I'm sorry,' and hurry over. I just heard from the last insurance company we've been waiting on, and we've been approved! As soon as we get the office in order, we can start seeing patients. Better get the appointment book out because we're officially in business."

I could hear the excitement in Trish's voice, and it worried me. Not because I wasn't looking forward to finally opening up our office but because I was afraid with this murder hanging over our heads that no one would show up. I felt like I was in *Treasure Island* and had been given the black spot—a sign of bad luck. Of death.

Everywhere I went, trouble seemed to follow.

"That's great news," I said, trying to keep my voice obnoxiously happy. "And yes, I'm sorry that I forgot. But I'll head over right now."

The therapy office was only two doors down from the town hall. I wondered if Trish would notice if I took a couple of extra minutes, considering I was already late.

Even as I thought it, though, I knew I couldn't do it. I'd abandoned Trish too often over the past few days, leaving her with the workload of getting the office up and running.

Besides, Sheriff Potts had things under control. She seemed to be everywhere, talking with everyone. At least, that was what I tried to convince myself of. I couldn't help but wonder if she'd managed to get anything useful. Because, when it came down to it, this town didn't trust her any more than they did me. Probably less, considering she didn't seem to have any ties to Amor. Take Debbie, for example. Even after that long interrogation at her house, she'd never told the sheriff about Kandy coming over early to help. Didn't trust the sheriff enough to be discreet and keep the information to herself—didn't trust the sheriff could keep Kandy safe.

Regardless, there was one more thing the sheriff didn't have going for her that I did.

My mom. Even if I wasn't a respected member of the community—yet—my mom certainly was. That connection had served me well when I was younger, and I was sure it still carried some weight.

My mom.

Another thing on a long list of items I'd forgotten. I was supposed to take the kids over for dinner tonight. She had called, complaining that it had been a week since she'd seen us, and that a murder was no excuse. I glanced at my phone, relieved when I saw I still had a couple of hours. Enough time to help Trish before running back home.

I was just passing a bike shop when I nearly ran into Sam, who was entering Main Street from a little side path that ran alongside the store.

"Oh, geez. Sorry, Sam. I didn't see you there." My heart was beating faster than it should have been, partly at being surprised by the mayor's presence and partly because Katie joined him a second later. And what looked like the entire town council. I didn't recognize most of them. James was there, but he looked annoyed by that fact.

"Maddie!" Sam looked much more pleased to see me today than he had the other night at Debbie's party. He had barely looked at me then, but of course I had just been on the end of Mrs. Bailey's tongue lashing. I wouldn't have known what to say either.

"It looks like you have all of town hall out here," I said, forcing a smile and hoping it came across as natural. As a therapist, I'd pretty much perfected the fake smile, but I hadn't been as confident in it recently.

"Nearly. Just taking the council out to the park to get to know the folks living there."

I blinked. "There are people living at the park?"

Katie nodded and spoke for the first time since I'd met her. "The homeless population was moved to a far corner of the park where no one would see them." She frowned. "That was Mrs. Bailey's doing." She glanced at Sam, and I noticed the quick shake of his head. Katie's smile returned as she turned back to me, but it was strained.

"The town gave them tents and supplies, but really it was just a way to placate them. I'm working on setting up an organization that will help them with interview skills, jobs, housing, that kind of thing. Sam and I thought it would be good if the town council met them personally, talked to them....saw that they are people. With stories. Not something to hide away and pretend doesn't exist." She threw another frown at the council members, who had walked around us and were making their way back to the town hall.

"I don't remember there being any homelessness when I was younger," I said, a little embarrassed that I hadn't known it was a problem. Of course, teenagers didn't generally pay attention to things like that.

Sam must have seen because he gave me a kind smile. "That was because we had hardly any to speak of. But times have changed, and so has the economy. We don't get snow, so it's a natural place for folks to migrate when they don't have shelter."

Katie's eyes lit up, like she'd just had an idea. "I've heard you are opening a therapy office soon. What would you say to my non-profit hiring you a couple of days a week to come out and talk with these guys?"

This was an unexpected twist in the conversation. "You want me to come out and have therapy sessions with the homeless?" It was actually a brilliant idea and would be helping the people who needed it most. Trish could run things back at the office on those days. Unless they needed two therapists at the camp, in which case we could shut the office down for those two days.

Looked like my luck was changing.

"That would be amazing. I need to talk to Trish about it first, but it seems like the kind of thing she'd enjoy."

Katie nodded, looking genuinely happy. It was amazing how something as simple as a smile could totally change someone's demeanor. Her expression held something else as well. Was it relief? That was interesting for someone who was supposedly being hounded by the sheriff. Katie didn't carry the same aura of stress and worry that Debbie had the last few days, and she didn't seem at all worried that she might be charged with murder.

"Katie," I said, wondering if I should even say anything. But I'd always had a hard time keeping my thoughts to myself. "I've heard that Sheriff Potts has been giving you a hard time. I'm sorry about that. Not exactly a warm welcome to Amor, is it?"

I expected Katie's expression to darken, to show her underlying emotions. To my surprise, she laughed and waved a hand through the air, like it was no big deal. "She's just doing her job. But it's silly to think me capable of something like murder. Even if Mrs. Bailey did deserve it."

Sam glanced at Katie, and I swore his expression held a warning. But Katie either didn't notice or didn't care, and she prattled on. "I know everything I say can be used against me and all that, but honestly, I'm just voicing out loud what no one else is willing to. From the moment I stepped into Amor, I've been ruffling feathers, and it's not the kind of thing that people around here are used to. Simply put, they don't like me. I suppose it's natural that everyone thinks I could be capable of doing Mrs. Bailey in."

I remembered Benji saying something about that. "By everyone, I'm assuming you mean town council?"

Katie laughed. "You'd have been a good cop. Psychologists are basically the same thing, except without the handcuffs, though, aren't they?" She paused. "No, you guys have it better. You get people to give up their darkest secrets in exchange for money. Not a bad racket, if you ask me."

What an interesting woman. And what was even more interesting was the fact that Sam was clearly in love with her. Even as he placed a hand on her lower back, like he was trying to steer her away from this conversation, his lips quirked up, his gaze never straying from her.

"I suppose you're right," I said. "We get away with asking very personal questions, and actually expect people to answer. But we also help an awful lot of people. If you ever need to someone to talk to, we're great at listening, and never divulge what has been discussed. Whatever is in your past will stay there."

Katie folded her arms over her chest and gave me an appraising look. "You've heard the stories about me, eh?"

When I hesitated, because I really didn't know much about Katie except the gossip that had been passed along, she laughed. "It's not like it's something I'm hiding. At least, not anymore, so we can skip the shrink session. No, my parents didn't care about me and left me to fend for myself. Yes, my car broke down in Amor as I was running from a cop. Yes, I lied about it. Yes, in my previous life, I stole and blackmailed people out of money. But that's not who I am, not really. I did what I had to do. And now I don't have to. Because Sam, and the rest of Amor, gave me a new start. A new life. A chance to become a better person."

Katie seemed genuine, and I found myself believing her.

"You've clearly taken that to heart," I said. "You've already done some amazing things to help the town. Tell me, how did Mrs. Bailey feel about your organization to help the homeless? It's a big project and would likely need to go through town council, correct?"

Now Katie's expression did darken. "You give me more credit than I deserve. I've only been here about a year, and that's not nearly long enough to do everything required to establish an entire organization. I started the process about six months ago." She paused. "I did bring it up in town council. Once. Last week. And Mrs. Bailey said the most horrible things about my friends who live in the park. Went on for a full fifteen minutes. No one could get her to stop, and they didn't want to have to use physical force. Not on someone like Mrs. Bailey. She'd probably have sued the town for assault."

Okay, now we were getting somewhere.

"Who else was at that meeting?"

It was Sam who answered this time. He seemed to be getting antsy, like he didn't feel comfortable with the direction this conversation was going in. "It was open to anyone who wanted to attend, but people are still in holiday mode. It was only the council, me, Katie, and some of the homeless."

"They come to your town meetings?"

"Just this one. They'd come so they could have a say when we discussed Katie's project. She'd spread the word on what she intended."

And then Mrs. Bailey had insulted all of them.

"I bet they were angry."

Katie released a humorless laugh. "You have no idea. Tension has been on the thick side around here. I hadn't realized Mrs. Bailey would be at that dinner party, so when we arrived and I saw she was there, I had to keep my distance, or I knew I was going to go crazy on the woman." Her eyes widened. "But I didn't. I never went near her."

No one had needed to. Because the murder weapon

hadn't required anyone to wield it. It had only been a matter of time until appetizers were served, and that would be that.

My phone buzzed with a text from Trish.

Shoot.

"Listen, I have to run. But it was very nice to meet you, Katie. I'll talk to Trish about therapy at the park. I think it's a wonderful idea, though."

Katie's expression cleared, and she smiled. "I look forward to discussing it further."

And then Sam took her hand, and they made their way back across the street to the town hall. It was only then that I noticed James watching us from near the entrance to the building. His lips were pulled down in a frown, as if he didn't like what he saw.

Well, that made two of us.

I spun around and hurried to our office building.

Debbie was right. This town was a powder keg. And it was about to explode.

12

It had been two days since my illuminating conversation with Katie. Two days I hadn't had time to go snooping around town playing detective, because I'd been too busy preparing the office for patients. And two days since I'd realized that maybe I didn't need to pretend I could solve Mrs. Bailey's murder. At this point, everyone seemed guilty to me, and in the time I'd spent getting everything lined up at the office, nothing bad had happened. No one had been falsely accused. The sheriff seemed to be taking her time, getting all the facts.

Of course, that was part of the problem—the facts.

I'd overheard several people say the sheriff would never get anyone to admit to anything, not when no one had wanted her there in the first place. Debbie herself had confided things to me that she hadn't told the sheriff.

But I didn't have time for all of that—extracting information from unsuspecting folks around town, all in the name of the better good.

Instead, I was currently covered in paint and wishing I had worn different shoes.

"Thanks for letting me drag them along," I told Trish. "The kids don't get enough practice with manual labor." I said this even as Flash groaned, dramatically cradling his left arm.

"It hurts. I think it's broken."

"You've been painting the wall for twenty minutes. I think you'll survive."

Flash turned up the panic a couple of notches. "No, really, I think I did something to it. I need a brace. And rest. And—"

"A computer?" I finished for him.

His cheeks darkened. "You don't know what it's like to miss a competition. I'm supposed to be there. Right now. I'm one of the biggest names attached to it, and my reputation is going to take a hit. They're going to think I somehow cheated on my other competitions, and now I've escaped with my earnings while I had the chance."

I rested my own paintbrush on the tray, amused. "You don't think they'll just assume you were busy?"

"Not for this one. It's the second biggest event of the year. Mom, I have to be there. My entire future is at stake."

Flash sounded so desperate, his eyes pleading, nearly in tears.

I couldn't hold out. It wasn't like he was making much

progress on the wall he was supposedly working on anyway.

"Fine," I said, releasing a sigh. "But if I let you go, you have kitty litter duty for the next three weeks."

"Deal."

"And trash duty."

"Fine," he said quickly.

Wow, I could really get him to agree to anything right now. This was fun.

"And—"

Flash seemed to have caught on because he held up a hand. "Kitty litter and trash. That's it." And then he grabbed his jacket and ran out the door. Even though he was joining the competition late, I had no doubt he would win.

Which begged the question, what was he doing with all his earnings? I'd never opened a bank account for him, which wasn't a bad idea now that I'd thought of it, and there hadn't been any mysterious packages showing up on the doorstep.

"That's not fair," Lilly said, placing her hands on her hips, forgetting she was holding a paintbrush. Paint splattered her leg as well as the plastic sheet she stood on. "Flash left. Does that mean I can too?"

Getting those two to help with anything was worse than dealing with James Rodney.

"Honey, we're opening next week, and we have a ton to do. We really need the help."

"But I really, really hate this," Lilly said. Things had looked like they might be getting better for her—our relationship—but it turned out that the only thing that seemed to bring Lilly out of her funk was helping investigate murders. And apparently the horrendous job we were doing on the walls of this office didn't count.

"I'll tell you what," I said. "You help Trish hang the banner outside that tells people we're now accepting appointments, and you can go home."

I hated being a pushover, but if I spent any more time arguing about the painting of the office walls—or the lack of painting, as it was—we were never going to finish.

"And promise to talk to me when I get home," I added.

Lilly had already begun to tear off her coveralls but was now frozen, one leg still stuck inside. "You mean a therapy session."

Yes, but I wasn't going to admit it. "I mean, we never talked about what happened while you were in Albuquerque. I just want to make sure you're okay."

Lilly gave me the most impressive teenage eyeroll I had ever witnessed. "Fine. Let's get this over with. Yes, I went to the party. Yes, it was awful. Yes, I have only been gone a few weeks, but everyone's moved on without me. No, I don't care. Yes, that's actually the truth, because everyone there was drinking and doing things I didn't realize they enjoyed doing. And if you ask me how I feel about that, I feel lucky. Lucky that isn't my life. But also betrayed. And it makes me realize that I don't know where I belong—I don't fit in anywhere, it seems. Oh, and, no, I don't like it here any more than I did on the first day. Except for the murder thing. That's made it a bit more interesting —bearable."

For once, I was speechless. I didn't know what to say— what to ask.

"Thanks, Mom." And then Lilly shook the coveralls free from her foot and sprinted out of the office.

Maybe I should look into getting the girl some therapy. Real therapy. That wasn't with me. And maybe sign her up for track. Put all her running to good use. The same thing that Benji had accused me of—running.

I supposed the apple didn't fall far from the tree.

I WAS CLEANING out the paintbrushes in the bathroom sink when I heard the office door open. I'd thought Trish had gone to pick up dinner from the diner and was meeting me back at the house. My arms were so tired from painting, I could barely hold the brushes, let alone a spatula. There would be no cooking from either of us for at least a couple of days.

"Trish," I called.

"No, it's Kandy."

I turned off the water and tapped the brushes against the side of the sink. When I entered the office lobby, Kandy was pacing back and forth. There was a restless energy bursting from her, reminding me of a caged tiger.

"Everything okay?" I asked, picking up a rag that had been unceremoniously thrown on the floor.

Kandy paused long enough to glance my way. Her eyes were troubled. No, it went deeper than that. They were haunted. "I saw your sign. That you're accepting appointments."

My heart leaped a little. Our first patient.

"Yes. Let me just grab a receipt or something to write on. I meant for our computers to already be set up, but it's going to end up being tomorrow morning. I'll enter you into the system as soon as—"

"No," Kandy interrupted. "I need it now."

I blinked a couple of times. "Oh. Now. Um...sure."

When I'd envisioned our first appointment, it had been in my beautifully decorated office with relaxing music, an environment that both calmed and reassured people that they were in a safe place.

Instead, I was covered in paint, the office was a mess, and I only had a couple of folding chairs. The rest of the furniture was arriving in two days.

"Would you like to go back into the office?" I asked awkwardly.

Kandy glanced toward the front door, her expression uneasy. "Yes, thank you." She paused, then looked back at me. "Even though this is kind of an impromptu thing and you're not officially open, you still have to observe patient confidentiality and all that, right?"

"Yes. Unless there is an immediate threat to someone's safety, not a word you say will leave this office."

"Okay." Kandy said it slowly, as if she wasn't sure she believed me. Or maybe it was that she was unsure if someone's safety was in jeopardy.

My heart beat fast in anticipation of what Kandy had to say to me. Was she about to confess to Mrs. Bailey's murder? If so, there would be nothing I could do about it. I was serious about what I'd said about confidentiality, even if it meant the murder went unsolved, and I'd always have to live under a cloud of suspicion, as would everyone else who had attended that party. The town always wondering who it had been.

Of course, if one of us were to be wrongfully convicted, well, that would be a different thing entirely.

I led Kandy into what would be my office, but the folding chairs weren't there. Nor were they in what would be Trish's office. Placing my hands on my hips, I did one more scan of the lobby, but when I still came up empty, I gave Kandy a sheepish smile.

"How does sitting on the floor sound to you? I have a couple of mats I put down to save my knees while painting."

Kandy returned my smile, though it was strained. "That would be just fine."

I pulled the mats into the back office and then gently touched the wall. The paint was dry. Once we were both seated, our legs stretched out in front of us, I said, "What's weighing on your mind, Kandy?"

She blew out a hard breath.

"The world." A pause. "Being married to James... It's had its challenges. He's not a kind person, Maddie. I mean, Dr. Swallows."

I bit back a smile. "Maddie is fine."

There was a fine line between wanting a patient to feel comfortable and also keeping it professional. But right then, we were sitting on the floor in a room that smelled of paint. Professional wasn't exactly in the cards for this session.

"Is he unkind to you?" I asked.

Kandy was quiet for a moment. "If you mean has he hurt me, no, absolutely not. He's never raised a finger against me. But he has hurt me. Emotionally. Mentally. He's broken me down. James can be charming, believe it or not. I do believe he loves me. And I love him. Deeply. But I gave up everything to live in Amor—be here with him. And I feel like I got the raw end of the deal."

"There must be a reason you've stayed. If it's fear that's keeping you rooted, I do have some resources I can give you." I had to keep my personal opinions to myself. Stay objective. Did I think Kandy should run as fast as she could in the opposite direction? If I were being honest, yes. But I couldn't tell her that.

Kandy shifted so that she could pull her knees into her chest. She looked so young, so childlike, in that pose. And maybe that was how James made her feel. "Our first year together was wonderful. I was happy. But then Mrs. Bailey came into our lives. And every day since then, yes, I've thought of leaving. I've been scared to even entertain the thought, but not for the reasons you're inferring. James has made me dependent on him. He didn't like the thought of me working, even though we don't have any kids. He wanted me home to make sure the house was clean, that dinner was ready. Honestly, I've become a 1950s housewife. It's gotten to the point that I read cookbooks because James is so particular. I'm constantly trying to find new recipes."

That supported what Debbie had told me earlier.

When I didn't respond right away, Kandy glanced away, like she was embarrassed. "I haven't worked in so long, I think I've forgotten how. My licenses have lapsed—I don't know if I'm employable."

"What type of work did you do before landing here in Amor?" I asked, shifting my weight. My legs were starting to fall asleep, but something was going on. Something big. And I needed to stay until Kandy felt safe leaving.

"I was a carpenter and a woodworker—I love the smell of wood. And working with my hands—it's the best feeling in the world." Kandy's lips twitched up as she let her thoughts drift to a happier time.

I wished I had a pen and paper to write things down, especially if I ever had another session with Kandy. Of course, this might be just a one-off. A chance for Kandy to get stuff off her chest.

"That must have been some romance to get you to leave everything behind and move here, your sister being your only other connection."

Kandy hesitated, like my statement might not be completely accurate.

"You weren't in love?" I asked.

"Oh, I was in love, all right," Kandy said quickly. "With the man James was. I know that man is still in there...somewhere."

Kandy's tone was so firm and resolute, it made me wonder if it was the other part of my statement that had given her pause. The part about her only other connection being her sister. If that were true—if there was someone else—why hide it? Unless it was someone she was embarrassed of and didn't want to be connected to.

I glanced at my phone. Trish would be back to the house by now. But I wasn't convinced that Kandy had gotten to the real issue that had led to her sitting on my office floor. "Why are you here, Kandy?"

Her gaze snapped up, and I saw that same haunted look she'd had when she'd first entered. Talking about James—those feelings were real. But they had been a distraction. Something to avoid telling me what was truly bothering her.

"I have a hypothetical situation for you."

The old "hypothetical situation" routine. A technique

that some patients used to be able to talk about hard things, but as if they were happening to someone else. A way to distance themselves from the pain and fear.

I nodded. "All right."

Kandy took another moment, sucking in long breaths, as if she were steeling herself for what she had to say. Mustering the courage. "Suppose you knew a person who had done something awful. I mean, really horrendous. Worst thing a person could do. It might have been an accident, could have been on purpose. There wasn't any way for you to know for sure, and you weren't even sure they knew themselves. Now, telling anyone about this awful thing they'd done would ruin their life. And since it might have been an accident, you don't want to spill their secret, only to discover there was a logical explanation behind it all. Besides, it's their secret to tell. What would you do?"

Something awful. Like accidentally killing someone with green chile?

"That's a very difficult position to be in," I said. "I can tell this has been weighing heavily on your mind. The question is, if you keep this secret, will it ruin *your* life? Will it forever color your interactions with not only this person but everyone around you? Always wondering if anyone else knows, as you do. Wondering if this person will do it again. Wondering if you should have told someone. Guilt has a way of gnawing through our protective layers that we place around ourselves and nestling in the deepest parts of our souls and hearts and our minds. Is that a burden you really want to carry?"

Kandy's gaze dropped, and I could tell she didn't love my answer. I was asking her to do probably the most difficult thing she'd ever do. Turn herself in.

"But what if it was an accident?" she whispered.

"Then you have nothing to fear, because the police will get to the bottom of it, and both you and your friend will have clear consciences. You'll be free of that extra weight you've been carrying."

Kandy nodded, her gaze still on the floor. "And if it wasn't an accident?"

I couldn't tell her that justice would be served and that she'd have a clear conscience. Because I knew all too well that she'd be carrying around a different kind of guilt after that. The guilt of sending someone you care about to jail, potentially ruining their life forever.

And if Kandy was indeed talking about herself, she knew very well what would happen if she had meant to murder Mrs. Bailey. The woman who had controlled everything that went on in their town—in Kandy's family. The way she'd kept James in check, and that probably translated to Kandy as well.

"Then the person will be able to get the help they need. There are therapists in prison. Doctors. Medication. It's very possible that it's not the end of your friend's life, but just the beginning."

Kandy thought on that, and I remained quiet. Sometimes the best thing a psychologist could do was nothing. Silence allowed someone the freedom to analyze who they really were, their choices, and to digest anything we might have discussed. An awful lot could happen internally when nothing was happening externally.

Usually this was when my patients started crying and thanking me. And Kandy did indeed thank me as she pushed herself up off the floor. But then she smiled and said, "You've helped me see things through a much clearer lens, Maddie. I've realized that I don't need to feel guilty for keeping things to myself. Because I'm not going to wonder all those things that you said might gnaw at me. I know this person won't do it again, so what good would it do to punish them for all eternity? It's not like prison would keep them from striking again, because they have no need to. What's done is done, and we can move on with our lives." She stretched her arms over her head. "Wow, therapy really is awesome. I'll definitely be giving you some referrals. How much do I owe you for our session?" Kandy pulled out her wallet.

I stared, my jaw slack. I was sure I looked like an idiot, but I had no idea how Kandy had reached that conclusion from what I'd just said. She had come into the office not liking how guilty she felt and had grasped at anything I said to justify her position. Anything that would take away the bad feeling.

As a medical professional, I was meant to do no harm.

But there was a very real possibility that I had just enabled a murderer.

That feeling solidified with the phone call I received before Kandy even had the chance to walk out the door.

It was Benji.

"Maddie, where are you? There's been another death. And you won't believe who."

13

The phone nearly fell from my grasp, and I barely managed to hold onto it.

"By death, do you mean..." I tossed a glance toward Kandy, who had paid for her session and was putting away her wallet. I lowered my voice. "Not a natural one?"

I couldn't bring myself to say murder. Not when Kandy was standing right there, and she'd practically admitted to killing Mrs. Bailey, whether it had been an accident or otherwise. If the killer herself wasn't even sure which it was, there was no telling what she was capable of.

"Not sure," Benji said.

I closed my eyes, not wanting to know the answer to my one-word question but knowing I needed it. "Who?"

"James Rodney."

This time, I did drop the phone. Kandy had just slung

her purse over her shoulder, and her features twisted in concern. "Everything okay?"

I snatched up my phone and told Benji I'd need to call him back. This was not the way this was supposed to be done. Kandy should be at home; the police would arrive. They'd break the terrible news, then ask a few questions. She'd sob. They'd determine if they believed her.

"Maddie?" Kandy said, touching my sleeve. I jumped back...a knee-jerk reaction.

I nodded, then morphed it into shaking my head. "I'm so sorry, Kandy. I know things were rough between you two, but for things to end like this. It isn't right."

As I spoke, I almost managed to convince myself that I didn't suspect Kandy. That this wasn't her way out of a loveless and stifling marriage. That there wasn't anything to gain by James's death. But if she'd already killed once, what was preventing her from doing it a second time?

Kandy's concern turned into panic. "What's happened? Is James okay?"

I tried to tell her, but the words stuck. When a second attempt didn't produce results either, I managed a head shake.

To say Kandy cried would be an understatement. The woman who had just spent a great deal of time telling me how difficult it was to be married to someone like James Rodney was now sobbing on the dirty floor. "With Mrs. Bailey gone, I thought things might be better between us. Thought the old James would come back—the man I married. The man who disappeared once Mrs. Bailey managed to get her tentacles on him." She rummaged in her purse and produced a bag of tissues. "I can't believe he's gone. This was supposed to be the start of something new."

I tried to find something to say but was still at a loss for words. That didn't happen very often.

As my silence persisted, Kandy carried on. "You know, he really was a wonderful man. Sure, James was stubborn and didn't like change. He could be gruff and off-putting. But he was also very sweet. Did you know that he gave me a foot massage every evening for our entire marriage? That was one of the things he'd promised me when we married, and he kept that promise."

My confidence that I was in the presence of a killer wavered. I knew that murderers could be charming when they needed to be, but if this was an act, Kandy should forget carpentry and head out to Hollywood.

I finally found my voice and moved toward Kandy. "I'm so sorry. If there's anything—"

A loud knock on the door stopped my words, but before I could open it, Sheriff Potts strolled in. She wasn't accompanied by her deputy this time, and I wondered if he was busy at the crime scene.

Music erupted from my phone again, and the sheriff raised an eyebrow, as if she were challenging me to not answer it. I glanced at the screen. It was Trish.

I answered it. "Hey, Trish. I know I'm taking a bit longer—"

"Oh my gosh, thank goodness you're all right. When I heard that James was dead and that they haven't been able to locate Kandy, all sorts of crazy scenarios started running through my head."

My gaze landed where Kandy still sat in a disheveled heap on the floor. "Uh, yeah. No, I'm good. You and the kids can eat without me. I'm just finishing some stuff up at the office."

"Okay. Just don't stay out too late with that hot friend of yours."

That momentarily distracted me from the horrifying events taking place around me. "I'm not with Benji right now."

"Ah hah! So, you admit that you think he's hot. Otherwise, your mind wouldn't have immediately landed on him."

I bit back a smile. "Focus, Trish. Why did you think I was with him?"

"Because he stopped by the house looking for you, and I told him where he could find you. It isn't right for you to string a man along like this, Maggie. Especially one as attractive and single as this one is."

Sheriff Potts tapped her wrist, as if she were wearing a watch, and gave me a pointed look. Time to end this potentially eternal phone call.

"No one is stringing anyone along. But hey, I have to get going. I should be home soon, though." I hoped.

The moment I pressed end, Sheriff Potts went into full angry-cop mode.

"I'm going to need to take both of you down to the station now."

"Potts, this woman just lost her husband," I protested.

The look I got after calling the sheriff by her last name ensured that it would not happen again.

"Yes," she said. "James Rodney is dead, and if it is murder, as I suspect it is, all evidence points to Kandy."

"What evidence? She has been here with me for the past hour and it's only been five minutes since we've heard the news of James's death."

It was strange being certain of the woman's guilt one moment and being convinced she was innocent the next. But the longer I argued on Kandy's behalf, the more I believed it. Kandy had not killed her husband.

Sheriff Potts frowned. "Then you two won't mind coming with me and giving me your statements." She turned toward the door, fully expecting us to follow. "Two murders in a week," she mumbled. "And they said it would be a quiet assignment."

THE SHERIFF'S office was in the basement of the town hall and shared the space with two jail cells. The office had a

separate entrance, accessible from a long walkway that
wound around the building. I had only been inside once—
when I was a teenager, we'd gone for a class field trip to try
to steer us away from a life of crime. It had worked, but
what they hadn't told me was that even if you don't go
looking for it, sometimes trouble comes to find you. Lately,
it seemed like wherever I went, a tragedy was sure to follow.

The office looked just as I remembered it—dingy,
depressing, but clean. At least it had that going for it.

"Sit," Sheriff Potts said, pointing to a chair by the door.
Kandy and I exchanged looks, wondering which one of us
she meant. When the sheriff glanced at me expectantly, I
dropped into the chair.

My phone went off and I pulled it out, glancing at the
screen. "Can I get that, or does it count as my one phone
call? It's my mom."

The sheriff seemed amused for the briefest of
moments before her frown returned. "You're not under
arrest. Take all the phone calls you need." And then she
led a terrified-looking Kandy into a back room.

I touched the green icon on my phone. "Hey, Mom."

"I'm at your house," she said, skipping all the pleas-
antries. "Where are you? We're getting worried, you know,
now that it's been confirmed there is a serial killer on the
loose. If you hadn't married Cameron, none of this would
have happened."

I tried to interject, wondering how she could have

possibly jumped to that conclusion, but she didn't allow it, steamrolling ahead.

"It's all about the energy we put out into the world. He's obsessed with killers, and look, he's brought one into your life. Poor James Rodney. I mean, none of us liked him, but you still have to feel bad about it, don't you?" She paused long enough to breathe. "I was worried about how all this murder business might be affecting the kids, but when I walked upstairs to check on them, it turns out they have a whole wall full of pictures and yarn and clues—it's like something you see in a movie. I must say, I'm concerned about how you're raising them—teaching them how to track down murderers and all that. It's not right, you know. Even if someone has to do it, as they claim, it should be an adult who—"

"Wait," I interrupted. And she wondered why I didn't stop by more often. "They're doing what?"

"Linking clues to help them solve the mystery of who's going around killing everyone. Now, I want you to know that your picture is up there too, but they assured me it is only for the purpose of being thorough. Because you were at the party. Not many of the clues point to you, so I don't think you have anything to worry about. They have a theory that it's someone who is going after town council. Like, they're doing a purging of those who have wrongfully controlled the town all these years."

I prayed the sheriff didn't visit the house before I could put a stop to things.

"Mom, tell them to pull it down. All of it. I'm not going to be home for a while. Sheriff Potts has a few questions for me, most likely to do with why I was spending the evening with Kandy, while unbeknownst to us, her husband was being—" Huh, I hadn't asked how he'd died. How unlike me.

"Slaughtered?" my mom so helpfully added.

"Sure. But I'll come home straight after, promise."

My mom *tssked*. "What you need is a lawyer. Don't you watch TV anymore? You always need a lawyer present, or she'll ask you a trick question and you'll end up in prison whether you did it or not."

"I doubt they do that in real life, Mom."

"Of course they do. I saw it in a documentary. It was really sad, and I couldn't finish it. A lady left behind her two children, and they had to be raised by the grandma for years until the police figured out they had the wrong person. I love you, Maddie. You know I do. But I'm just not in any condition to have teenagers again."

"Mom, I'm not going to prison, and you aren't going to be an insta-mom, okay?" Even though Sheriff Potts and Kandy were nowhere in sight, I said, "Look, the sheriff needs me. I'll talk to you when I get home."

"Okay, but you'll need to pick up food on your way. Your dinner was getting cold, so I helped myself. You don't eat enough, you know. So busy all the time, even when you don't technically have a job. Rest more—relax. Maybe go on a vacation."

I loved my mom. I really did. But there were times when a person had to hang up on the people they loved most.

"I'll think about it, Mom. Love you. You're fantastic. See you in a bit." And I hit the red icon.

"Did you just hang up on your mom?" Sheriff Potts said, walking out of the back room with a shaking Kandy following just behind her.

"Trust me, you would have too." One glance at Kandy told me this wasn't going to be just a friendly chat. "What did you do to her?" I demanded, rushing over to my new friend and patient.

Because yes, that was what we were now. Friends. I thought. Maybe. It was kind of hard to tell, given the circumstances.

"We did nothing but talk. She is a bit concerned, though, that her husband died of tetrahydrozoline poisoning. Just a got a call confirming its presence in James's blood and urine. It was an exorbitant amount—overkill, if you don't mind the pun."

"I do."

Kandy began shaking even harder, her skin clammy, her face pale. "I'm going to be sick," she whispered. I stepped back just as she ran for the nearest trash can and emptied her stomach into it.

I didn't know what tetrahydrozoline was, but whatever it was, Kandy hadn't done it. I was sure of it.

"You can't do this—accuse someone of killing her

husband just because it's convenient. Kandy was with me. I can vouch for her."

"So you've said. But Kandy knows her husband's habits better than anyone and emptying a bottle of eye drops into his favorite mug wouldn't have been hard. It's doubtful he would have noticed before filling it with hot water for his five-thirty tea. If nothing else, James Rodney was a creature of habit. For the time being, Kandy needs to stay here."

My heart stalled. "You mean, you're arresting her? I'm telling you, she didn't do it."

"How do you know that, Ms. Swallows?" The sheriff took a step closer. "How are you so sure? I don't suppose you know something that you haven't told the police. Because that would be withholding evidence."

I thought back to the video of Kandy arriving at Debbie's house early to help with the food preparation. And of her sneaking around the house when I'd come to talk with them. Her immediate need to have a therapy session to ease her conscience. And now her unloving husband had been poisoned, when it was she who knew exactly what mug he'd use, and when.

No, I had nothing I needed to tell the sheriff, but it did have me questioning my own ability to read people. I was usually so good at it, and yet I had repeatedly made excuses for Kandy's actions. Even when the evidence was so damning and, I had to admit, my belief in her innocence had wavered more than a time or two. But I always came back to the thought that she hadn't done it.

Why?

It wasn't only the sheriff who was missing something. And I couldn't allow something like getting myself arrested to interfere with figuring out what it was.

14

Sheriff Potts steepled her fingers and watched me for longer than necessary. Probably a police tactic to try to get me to talk—people hated silence. I'd learned that way back when I had been a therapist, before I'd gotten the job at the university with Cameron.

I felt the same urge to speak but forced myself to sit quietly. The sheriff wasn't going to pull one over on me today.

"A therapy session," the sheriff finally said.

Maddie: 1, Sheriff: 0.

Her gaze seemed to bore into me. "That was it, huh?" It was so hard not to look away. "Funny, I didn't think your office was open quite yet."

"Not officially. But we sometimes make an exception."

"Like, say, for someone who has just experienced a traumatic event? Maybe murdering their husband, then realizing what they'd done. Regretting it." That was what I got for talking, and it hadn't even been a direct question.

Maddie:1, Sheriff:1.

"Unfortunately, I can't divulge the topic of discussion," I said. "Confidentiality, you know."

"Yes, I do know. I've met many therapists who claimed I shouldn't have access to information during an ongoing murder investigation. But that's the thing. It's ongoing. And the murderer could still be a threat to the town, especially considering that he or she has already struck twice. So, you can save your little confidentiality spiel, because it doesn't apply when there is a major threat to the safety of these people."

The sheriff was correct, but Kandy wasn't a threat. She'd never told me she'd hurt anyone—hadn't said she'd killed anyone either. "I don't believe she's a threat to anyone, and she has never divulged anything to make me feel otherwise. So, if you'll excuse me, I think we're done here. Unless there's something you wanted to ask me that doesn't have to do with Kandy."

Sheriff Potts shook her head and released a long breath. "We're on the same side here, Ms. Swallows. At least, I hope we are. You do want your name permanently scratched off my suspect list, don't you?"

"I don't know why you still think I could have anything to do with Mrs. Bailey's murder. You have no more on me than you do the mayor." Which was nothing.

"I'd agree with that," the sheriff said. "Which is why I'm

questioning him next, considering he's the last one to have seen James Rodney alive." My shock must have been obvious, because she gave me an amused smirk. "Trust me when I say that I haven't crossed anyone off my list."

This was why I should stick to my daytime profession. But I wasn't going to admit as much to Sheriff Potts. I folded my arms over my chest. "Then how can you hold Kandy when you still suspect five other people? Myself not included, of course."

"That makes six others. And you should be happy that it's her sitting in my jail cell—grateful that all fingers point to her right now, and not you." The sheriff paused. "You have two children, don't you?"

My blood froze, and I threw the best glare I could muster. "Is that a threat?"

Sheriff Potts had the decency to look shocked at the accusation. "No, of course not. I'm just saying, sometimes keeping your head low and allowing the police to do their job is the safest course of action."

More like the sheriff didn't want anyone interfering or questioning her. That was something I'd learned over the years when working with the police in a few different cases where I'd had to report abuse that my patients were experiencing—or instigating.

"I'm sorry, but I don't think you have all the facts. Kandy is innocent."

I didn't mention that I didn't think I had all the facts either—that I had no reason to believe Kandy was free of any wrongdoing, other than women's intuition. And I didn't think that was admissible in court.

"Can I go now?" I asked, tired of dealing with this—tired of not being able to trust anyone. I never should have left Albuquerque.

That wasn't true.

I had needed to get out of there. But maybe I should have chosen someplace other than my hometown.

Sheriff Potts studied me, her gaze making me uncomfortable. "I didn't call you in here because I thought you guilty." I was shocked at her admission and waited for her to continue.

She didn't.

"So, you just wanted to spend some quality time with your favorite small-town therapist?" I tried to use a teasing tone, but the joke fell flat.

"I wanted to figure out if you knew anything that I didn't. From what I gather, people don't like you."

Ouch.

"But," she continued, "from the little I've seen over the past few days, they trust you. That gets people to let their guard down. Talk about things that maybe they wouldn't normally. I don't know if it's because, as a therapist, you're good at reading people or you know the right questions to ask. But whatever it is, I don't have it. I'm neither liked nor trusted here in town. People don't think I can keep them safe." She shrugged. "Maybe they're right. Just this week, two people have died. And I'm no closer to figuring out who the killer is than I was the night of your party."

Sheriff Potts clamped her lips shut, like she hadn't meant to tell me all that. But to my surprise, her lips turned up, and she released a small chuckle. "See what I mean? I shudder to think you are the killer, with that gift of yours. Getting us all to tell you our secrets before you strike."

Yes, that was a terrifying thought, for me included.

"But you don't think I did it. You don't even think Kandy did it."

The sheriff gave a slow shake of her head. "No, I don't. But people need to see that I'm doing something—that I'm making progress. So what, I know how each of the victims was murdered. That's as far as the lab reports have gotten me. Beyond that..."

As her voice trailed off, I couldn't help but feel sorry for the sheriff. Like I wanted to help her. Maybe I wasn't the only one with a special gift to make others want to do things.

But the only evidence I had thus far all pointed to Kandy. I couldn't very well hand that over to Sheriff Potts.

"I wouldn't mind working together," I said, my words slow. "You know, you give me information you receive in the coming days, and I do the same." In the coming days. Meaning I didn't need to hand over evidence I'd already gathered—or more like, evidence my children had gathered—only what I received in the future. I loved technicalities. "Nothing that comes from a therapy session, though. That I can't do."

Sheriff Potts had that look again. The one where she was trying to figure out the right thing to do. Or more like, wondering if she was really the type of person to bend the rules. She didn't want to, I could see that in her conflicted expression. But I could also see the desperation. Something else was driving her. Sheriff Potts had been born a rule follower. Whatever was tormenting her, it was probably the thing that had brought her to Amor in the first place.

"I'll only share what I think might help you notice the things that I'm not seeing. I'm not going to give you everything I've got."

Sheriff Potts could try to justify it all she wanted, but she knew even that was against the precious rules that she loved. If I were being honest, I used to be like that. But the incident that had brought me to Amor had changed me. Made me realize that the rule followers didn't always come out on top. Not when money or power or reputation were on the line. And I could bet that whatever had brought the sheriff here had something to do with one of them, if not all three.

"The thing about clues, Sheriff, is that it is almost impossible to tell which ones mean something and which ones are merely there to throw us off the scent."

Sheriff Potts frowned. "You want everything."

"Every single little thing."

"Or what?"

I knew I was pushing the boundary, and it might scare the sheriff off. I could be left with nothing, plus a jail cell for extortion. But we couldn't risk getting the wrong person. Both for justice and because I had brought my family here. To a place that I had thought was one of the safest places in the country.

Nothing interesting ever happens in Amor.

I wasn't generally a superstitious person, but I was pretty sure I had jinxed this whole thing into existence.

"Or you may get the wrong person. And that's the last thing you want. Trusting a complete stranger who tends to stick her nose where it doesn't belong is worth the risk, don't you think?"

The sheriff snort-laughed and didn't bother covering it up like she usually did. It was good to see there was a real human being under that uniform and all those frowns she tended to throw at me.

"Fine. But if you so much as step out of line, this whole thing is off."

I stood, twisting my back and getting it to pop, then gave Sheriff Potts my best serious expression. "My dear sheriff, we're already so out of line, we can't even see it anymore."

15

"Mom!"

Flash and Lilly thundered down the stairs the moment I stepped through the door.

"Hey, guys. How you holding up?"

"Great." Flash was sporting a wide grin, and even Lilly was smiling. It was a miracle. Too bad it took two people dying to make that smile appear. I wondered if I should be worried, but then decided to just be grateful that Lilly and I were on speaking terms again.

"We made a timeline of where everyone was at each moment, both leading up to the death of Mrs. Bailey and after, based on what we've overheard people say here and in town," Lilly said.

When I gave them a questioning glance, Lilly folded her arms, defiant. "What? You and Trish talk loud, and

Grandma knows everything about everyone. She's been filling us in on the details we missed."

Oh, I was sure she had. My mom might say that she was concerned about my children's obsession with solving these murders, but she was just as bad.

"And what have you concluded, my little sleuths?"

My kids exchanged a look, then Lilly nodded, as if she were giving Flash permission to tell me something.

He turned to me. "That we need to know where everyone was during the time of the second death. I jumped onto my computer—I won't tell you which site for your own protection—and they updated the report on James Rodney. They say that he died around seven p.m. Same time as Mrs. Bailey. He died of tetrahydrozoline poisoning—it's commonly found in redness-reducing eye drops. Now, James Rodney didn't ever cook his own food— barely set foot in the kitchen—according to the diner owner, Melinda. Someone probably prepared his tea for him."

Flash must have seen my dubious expression, and said, "Grandma took us out for fries and ice cream after dinner. Anyway, since both his and Mrs. Bailey's deaths took place in the dining room, we think it's possible that their killer is the same person. I know, not the same methodology. But we're just pulling on threads at this point, wondering which one will make the whole thing unravel. We know that Kandy was with you, but we don't know how long the tea was sitting out before James Rodney drank it, or even how long it takes for the symptoms to set in, so we can't let her off the hook quite yet."

I had tried so hard to keep my kids away from this kind of thing. I had always hated it when Cameron talked to them about some of the more gruesome aspects of his work, and he'd always cut himself off when I gave him *the look*. They had been far too young to know of the awful things that people can do—the monsters people could become.

But the kids were proud of what their dad did. They saw that because their dad chose to go into the minds that no one else wanted to, he could help the police catch the very people they were fascinated by. In spite of how often I complained about my ex-husband's ego, he had done some real good in the world, and my kids were smart enough to see it. And they saw the chance to do the same thing themselves.

I felt guilty about it, and yet proud. The sheriff wouldn't understand, though.

"I know you want to help," I told them. "And I think you're on the right track. You would make excellent detectives. But it stops here. Take down the pictures and the timeline and everything in your room. This is a job for the police. Not two teenagers."

Lilly and Flash didn't move.

"You're not the police either, you know," Lilly said, folding her arms and jutting out her chin. "And yet you've been going around, talking to people. Trying to figure it out. Because you don't trust the sheriff to get it right."

Using my own words against me. I hated it when they did that.

"I've been asking around, sure. But I'm a therapist. That's what I do. Figure out motivations, inner thoughts, what drives people to do the things they do."

I realized I was defending myself to my child—even though Lilly was closer to being a woman than a child, and that thought frightened me. I pursed my lips.

"My money is on Katie," my mom said, piping up from where she was sitting at the kitchen table. I glanced over my shoulder at her. She had been so quiet, I'd forgotten she was still there, snacking while listening to us going back and forth, like she was enjoying the show.

"Katie had no reason to hurt Mrs. Bailey or James Rodney," I said. "If anything, she needs to be more careful because of her past; she wouldn't be reckless. Besides, she used to con money out of people—she didn't kill them."

My mom nodded slowly. "Sure. But what if she was trying to help her new boyfriend out? What if she saw how frustrating it was, no one listening to the mayor? Treating him like he was a nuisance they could sweep aside. His vote meaning nothing with Marci and James running town council. Love can make people do crazy things."

Great. Now we were the murder-solving equivalent of *The Incredibles*, a family out on a mission to save the world.

Except instead of a husband, I had a geriatric mother tagging along for the ride.

"Thank you for your input, Mom. I will take it into consideration."

Mom's lips pulled down into a frown. "Look, I know you think I'm crazy. Nosy. That there is no possible way I could figure out something you can't—you feel the same way about your children. But if you would at least consider that we could be helpful, you might find Kandy on the outside of that jail cell a lot sooner than you think."

"I don't think I'm smarter than you, Mom. But it is my job to protect my family. I am all these kids have. And with Dad out of the picture, I'm all that you've got too. So excuse me for getting a bit nervous when my family wants to go out and find a murderer." I released a sigh and rubbed my forehead, feeling a headache coming on.

"New place, same mom," Lilly muttered as she ran up the stairs. Her bedroom door slammed.

Flash gave me a sad look, like he was disappointed in me. As if I were a child who had let him down. And then he followed his sister up the stairs.

"They're good kids, you know," my mom said, chewing on a fry. "You don't want to blow it with them like I did with you. It's a miracle you returned home after all these years. With those two, you might not be so lucky."

Shame.

Guilt.

"But Mom, a murder investigation?"

I knew I'd inadvertently been pushing them away, not knowing how to keep them close. But there were some lines a responsible mother didn't cross. Like allowing your children to hack into government files or film people without their permission, all in the name of family time.

"They've already helped you—they're good at what they do. Why don't you let them fly a little instead of tethering them to their perch? You'd be surprised what you can see with a bird's eye view." My mom pushed back her chair and stretched. "Now, if you'll excuse me, I'm to the point where I have to go to bed early or risk being stuck in that hard chair all night."

"I'll drive you," I said, reaching for my keys.

My mom shook her head. "Those kids need you right now. I'll be fine walking. I might be old, but I'm not crippled."

I wanted to point out that she was getting there. She'd developed a limp since I'd last seen her—it had been so long. The only times she'd been able to see her grandkids had been when she'd driven up to Albuquerque once every couple of years.

More shame and guilt.

Just because my mom and I had never seen eye to eye hadn't meant that I needed to keep the kids from her.

That was my fault, and I was determined not to allow history to repeat itself.

. . .

I SAT at the kitchen table. Alone. The sun was just beginning to rise when Trish sleepily descended the stairs, her hair matted and mascara smeared. I was pretty sure she was wearing the same clothes she'd worn the previous day.

"What happened to you?" I asked. My words slurred together, and I realized I probably looked just as bad as Trish, if not worse. I hadn't been able to sleep, but not for lack of trying. Thoughts had pulsed in and out, unrelenting.

The conversation with my mom ran on repeat.

And the way my kids had looked at me—like I had betrayed them. Like I didn't appreciate all they had done. Didn't see how hard they were trying to help.

Maybe they were right. Maybe I had been working so hard to undo the damage their father had done that I had made things worse.

Then the thought that maybe they were better off with their father swirled through the fog. I allowed myself to consider the possibility that rather than damage our children, Cameron had helped them see the world in a different way. Made them stronger. More resilient. Problem solvers. People watchers.

Trish slumped into the chair across from me and rested her forehead on the table. "My mind wouldn't shut off. For one, there have been two murders this week, in a town you pitched to me as being the ideal community to meet a good guy. And oh, yeah. You said I wouldn't have to deal with the bureaucracy and chaos of a large city. You said this town needed us. I like being needed. But not once did you ever say anything about Amor being the murder capital of the world."

I gave her a weak smile. "Uh...sorry? And I promise I won't ever beg you to follow me anywhere ever again. I swear I don't know what's happened to this town. It wasn't like this when I was a kid."

Trish raised her head slightly, her eyes half closed. "Before you got home, your kids were telling me of a couple of theories they had. One was that these murders were done by the same person. Yes, they both happened in the dining room, but that doesn't matter much. People spend a lot of time eating. It's a popular place to be."

"I agree. Two members of town council have been killed—I think that's the better link."

Trish raised her head high enough to rest it in her hands. "And there are five more council members. Do you think they are in danger?" She seemed worried by the thought, her eyes still closed, but her forehead scrunched in concern.

I'd been so worried about my family's involvement, the thought had never occurred to me. And I wondered if the sheriff had missed it as well.

"I don't know everyone who is on town council," I told Trish. "I think my mom mentioned that Sam's younger sister, Ruby, is on there. She's the most recently elected. But as for the other four, I have no idea."

"Well, now's the time to find out," Trish said, moving to stand but stumbling as she did.

I smiled as I stood and moved to help her. "I think you better go back to bed and let me take care of it." I placed my hands on Trish's shoulders and turned her toward the stairs. "I'll let you know if I find out anything."

To my surprise, Trish didn't protest. Didn't look like she had the energy, even if she'd wanted to. She merely nodded and stumbled up the stairs.

Yes, I could call Sam and find out quickly. But I hadn't known him all that well when we were younger, and it seemed odd for me to call him out of the blue at seven-thirty on a Saturday morning.

I did know someone who knew everything about everyone, though. You know, other than my mom.

16

"Thank you so much, Benji. I really appreciate you helping me out like this. But you could have just told me their names over the phone." I stuffed a too-big bite of pancake into my mouth.

He threw one of his easy grins my way and cut his omelet with his fork and knife. How polite people do it. Not savages, like I was, apparently. But really, I had forgotten how delicious breakfast at the diner was.

Melinda walked up with a pitcher of water in hand. "You're going to choke if you keep eating like that," she said, refilling my cup. I'd had orange juice, and now the water in my cup was tinted orange. But I didn't say anything, because in high school, Melinda had been one of those people everyone was afraid of. Not that she was violent or anything like that. But just...ornery. Mean-spirited.

Now that I had years of training and working with people like Melinda, I felt sorry for her. She was compensating for something. Maybe life hadn't been fair, maybe her family hadn't been as great as they had seemed back then, and she'd felt she needed to take it out on everyone else. Frankly, I was surprised that she had chosen to take over her family's diner. She'd always acted like she resented it. It made sense on some level, though. If she couldn't be in control of the awful parts of her life, she could at least be in control of this.

But just because I felt like I was starting to understand why Melinda was the way she was didn't mean that I wanted to seek out her forked tongue.

Melinda took Benji's empty cup and returned with a new one. She gave him a smile that seemed like much more than just a smile. Almost like those two had history. But when I looked at Benji, he didn't seem to notice.

"Thanks," he told her around a mouthful of food. And then kept eating.

Melinda glanced at me, like it was my fault, her smile morphing into a frown, and she stalked off.

Benji may not have noticed Melinda's obvious attempt at flirtation, but he did notice my orange-hued water. "Here, you can have mine." He gave me an amused smile as he slid his cup over. Orange juice. A full cup.

Melinda had refilled mine with water on purpose.

I beat down the annoyance. "You really didn't have to

do all this," I said, taking a swig of the juice. "I didn't mean to wake you on your day off."

Benji waved a hand through the air. "Darling, I'm never off. We don't have any of those twenty-four-hour emergency service places like you have in the big city. Things break, and I'm the one who needs to fix them, day or night, seven days a week."

"Sounds stressful."

"It can be. But I also like keeping busy. Otherwise, I have too much time on my hands, and we both know that nothing good comes from that."

I felt heat rush into my cheeks as I thought of all the stunts we'd pulled as teenagers. The more I thought about it, the more I realized how lucky I was to be a mom of two teenagers who enjoyed trying to help me solve murders rather than sneaking out in the middle of the night to trespass who knew where. Not that Benji and I had caused too much trouble. Just the local golf course now and then, armed with blocks of ice that we would ride down the biggest hill they had—killing the grass as we went, we later discovered.

Benji pushed his empty plate away from him and watched me. Studied me. His gaze made me nervous, which was a first, and I focused on my sausage.

"You really think someone is targeting town council?"

I gave a hesitant nod. "Could be. From what my mom says, people aren't too happy with how things have been going the past couple of years."

"That's true. But most of the town council are good folks who just happen to be outnumbered or bullied into votes they don't agree with. Sam's younger sister, Ruby, is on the council."

"She was the only one I could remember my mom mentioning. Who are the other four?"

"Darci Abrams. Hank Peters. Tyler Baker and Crystal Simmons."

Those names meant little to me. I thought I remembered Crystal as being a few years older than me. And I had gone out with Tyler on a date once, but the only memory I had from it was that he'd smelled like tuna fish.

"Do you have their addresses? I know we don't know for sure if their lives are in danger, but I really don't want to take any chances. They should be warned to be careful." I thought of Flash's comment about both of the murders taking place in the dining room. "Especially while eating. No dinner parties for the time being."

"I'll do you one better," Benji said. "I'll go with you."

The bell over the diner door jingled, and I glanced back to see Trish entering with Flash and Lilly. The kids spotted me and walked over.

"Hey, Mom," Flash said. Lilly still looked as if she were giving me the silent treatment. "Trish said you had come here for breakfast. I know what you said. But we want to help."

"This must be the infamous duo I keep hearing about,"

Benji said with a grin. He stood. "I think there's enough room if we all squeeze."

I eyed the booth where we sat. Sure, if Flash was sitting on my lap, maybe. But if it would get me back on speaking terms with Lilly, I was willing to squeeze in a little. Before leaving for breakfast, I had knocked on her door, wanting to talk. Whether she had been sleeping or not, I didn't know, but there hadn't been an answer.

"You all had slept in, or I would have invited you," I said, moving as close to the wall as I could.

"It's all right, we're not hungry," Trish said. She glanced at the kids. "At least I'm not. I bet these two could eat three breakfasts and still be hungry."

That finally got a reaction out of Lilly. "I told you, it's all Flash." She seemed insulted that Trish would think of her as having a large appetite.

"It's true. I could eat again," Flash said, sliding in next to me.

I threw a questioning glance at him. "You've already eaten?"

"Sure. Grandma came over and cooked breakfast. I heard the door slam when you left, and she arrived about five minutes later."

Dread settled in my stomach. "Where is Grandma now?"

"Right here," her voice rang out, approaching from behind me. "Do you always leave the kids alone like this? I mean, honestly, Maddie. You're worried about the kids adjusting to a new town, but then you constantly leave them to their own devices. What did you expect would happen? Parenting is like prison. You have to put in the time."

"Grandma!" Lilly said.

"Bad analogy, Mom. And these two spend most of their time on their electronic devices. They don't even notice when I'm home." I glanced at the kids. "That will change when school starts up again."

"All I'm saying is that some family time is what these kids need. Go out to a park and fly some kites, have a picnic, laugh a little."

"I don't eat on the ground," Lilly said.

Flash looked at his sister like she was crazy. "I'll eat anywhere you want me to."

"Thanks for the parenting tip, Mom," I said. "I'll see what I can do. In the meantime, Benji and I have some business to attend to."

"Perfect. That's something we're all interested in." My mom looked around at the group, like she was appraising us. "I suppose it will look a little silly if we're all traipsing about together." She turned to Trish. "Why don't you go work on the office? You know, let us have some family bonding time." She turned to me. "Let me know who you need to visit, and we can split the list."

Trish's jaw slackened, and her expression seemed to morph between shock and anger.

"Mom, Trish is part of this family now. She's like the

sister you never gave me. Besides, you aren't coming on this field trip either. It's something of a sensitive nature, and I don't need to bring the entire clan." I noticed Lilly's eyes narrow slightly and knew I needed to do something to try to make amends with her. "I appreciate you wanting to help, but this time it's just the kids. Like you said, family time."

"B-but I am family."

"I know you are, but sometimes we need a little alone time, that's all. You got to have breakfast with them, and now we're going to go on a walk around town. Get to know it a little better."

My mom straightened. "No investigating? Maddie, you know I only walk when I need to—I have to have a purpose. Otherwise, you're just tiring out your feet for nothing."

"That's why I hadn't invited you—I knew you wouldn't like it."

She sniffed. "Well, all right, then. But I expect you all to stop by my house for lunch. After your *walk.*"

I wasn't sure I could handle any more of my mom today, but it seemed like it was the only option to keep all of us happy. "It's a deal. But we can't stay for long. Trish and I really do have a lot to do on the office. We've already booked appointments for next week, and we can't keep our public waiting."

My mom's expression softened. "I'm glad you came

back with the kids, Maddie. It's been hard having you live away for so long."

"I know. And I hope to stay."

Trish glanced at me in surprise, and I had to admit, she wasn't the only one shocked to hear those words coming out of my mouth. With all that had been going on, the rough transition with the kids and the murders and the gossiping neighbors—I hadn't been sure I'd make it another week. But the kids needed stability, and if Trish and my therapy office was successful, I could see us making a home here.

As soon as we cleared out all the murderers, of course. Hopefully sooner than later.

17

"Who's left on the list?" I asked Benji. He was talking to Flash about some video game or other and had gotten distracted. I wasn't even certain we were walking toward anyone's house at this point, taking turn after turn, seemingly at random.

Benji glanced toward me mid-laugh. Those two seemed to be getting along well. Even Lilly was warming up and was joining their conversation. As far as I knew, she'd never played a video game in her life, but Benji had that effect on people. They naturally gravitated toward him and wanted to be a part of whatever he was doing.

"Tyler Baker and Darci Abrams," he said, looking up as if consulting a virtual checklist in the sky. His gaze returned to me. "I suggest leaving Darci for last."

"Why's that?"

Benji raised an eyebrow like that was something I

should already know. "She's Kandy's sister. I figured we'd want to ask additional questions—see what she knows about Kandy and James's relationship. If they'd ever talked about someone who might not be happy with town council. The kind of stuff that Kandy might be hiding."

Kandy's sister. Why hadn't I thought of speaking to her earlier, even before I knew she was on town council? Seemed like Mrs. Bailey and the Rodney family had created a dynasty of sorts—their own little bubble who would all vote the same way. I wondered if Darci was anything like James and Mrs. Bailey. If so, she might very well be the next victim. Our murderer seemed to have a "type."

"We could save her for last, but I wonder if the longer we put it off, the more likely she is to know we're on our way. Word travels fast around here."

Benji smiled. "Yes, it does. Which means that she already knows to expect a visit from us. We probably should have stopped by her place first."

I didn't tell him that there was no way I could have known that, because I hadn't known who Kandy's sister was in the first place. Instead, I returned his smile. "As it stands, let's leave Darci for last. I too think we'll need to spend some extra time at her place."

Lilly had her phone out, recording everything as we walked. I seized the opportunity to try talking to her.

"I'm sorry about last night. I know you two are just trying to help."

Lilly didn't lower the phone. "Then why won't you let us?"

"Because I love you. And I'm responsible for your safety."

"Dad—"

"Dad talked to you about his research and people he'd visited in prison. He didn't actually take you. He never put you in harm's way."

Lilly stopped mid-step and turned toward me. "We're not in danger. And you wanting to go do things on your own without telling anyone what you're up to—that's more worrisome. Flash and I—we just want to feel like our world isn't falling apart around us. And we finally found something we enjoy doing together. Solving mysteries, unraveling clues. That's interesting. Decorating your office and inhaling paint fumes? Not as fun. Grandma gets it. Why don't you?"

Yes. Grandma. The fun one. The one who didn't respect anyone's personal space. There was a reason I'd had to move across state.

"Your grandma and I… We never had a great relationship. I suppose it was similar to what you and I have right now—and that scares me. I don't want to push you away. I don't want you to feel like you have to run away the moment you turn eighteen, just to put some distance between us. But I don't know how to give you what you want and do what's best for you at the same time."

Benji and Flash were nearly to the end of the street

when Benji glanced back and realized we were no longer with them.

"How about letting me make decisions once in a while?" Lilly said. "I didn't have a choice in where I lived, or with who, when you and Dad split up."

When Cameron and I had divorced, it hadn't even been a matter of discussion. Between Cameron's position as department head at the university and all the travel he did for his self-promotion, there had been no way he could have the kids stay with him.

I'd never stopped to think that the kids wouldn't see it that way—that they didn't have enough information to see the logical conclusion.

"I'm sorry," I said. "I really am. None of this has been fair."

Lilly blew out a hard breath. "Just trust us once in a while, okay?" And then she jogged to catch up with the boys.

Trust. That was a hard one to come by these days. But I needed to try.

"MADDIE LAWSON," Tyler said, looking me up and down. I wanted to hide my children behind Benji. I hadn't remembered him being quite so creepy. "It's been a long time. And I hear you're single now."

If there was another target for the murdering vigilante,

this was their guy. He was tall, thin, and had an overbite. And he still smelled like tuna fish.

"Yup. Been a while," I said, taking a step backward. "Just wanted to stop by and let you know that it's possible a murderer is targeting people on town council. Thought you should know. Only eat what you prepare yourself. And...yeah. Take care."

I turned to usher my kids out, but Benji didn't follow.

"Tyler, I seem to remember you and Maddie being an item. Is that right?"

My kids stopped in their tracks. Flash's expression was one of disgust, but Lilly's? It was one of pure joy.

"Really, Mom." She grinned. "I think we need to hear more about this."

I threw a glare at Benji, and he grinned too.

Tyler puffed out his chest a bit. "Yeah. I remember this one time, your mom and I went out to see this fantastic horror movie, and she couldn't keep her hands off me. Held on tight to the very end."

Heat coursed through my face. I had to get out of there. Now.

"It was one date, Tyler. And I hadn't known it was going to be a horror movie. *The Wedding* sounds like it should be a romantic comedy, and you didn't bother to correct me."

"Mom hates horror movies," Flash said. "Won't watch ones that make you jump even a little."

"That's because everything makes her jump," Lilly said.

She still wore a smile that told me she was loving every minute of my obvious discomfort. Hopefully she would consider us even after this and we could go back to how things used to be. Before they had met Tyler.

Tyler's expression darkened. "It was supposed to be more than one date, but you turned me down. Repeatedly. Pretended we didn't have something special. Instead, you preferred to be a third wheel to Benji and his dates. Everyone knew you were desperate to be with him. And you chose the role of mistress, rather than be with someone who would actually give you the time of day."

Okay, this just went from bad to bury-me-alive.

"You had a thing for Benji?" Flash asked, delighted.

Lilly was now the one who looked disgusted. "You were the mistress?"

"You cannot believe a word that man says. And Tyler, I changed my mind. Eat as much as you can, from whoever will give it to you. And you should definitely drink tea."

I turned and hurried out as quickly as I could, not bothering to check if anyone was following. Lilly was right. We never should have come to Amor. Maybe there was a small town in northern Alaska that needed my help. Convincing Trish to move our office might be a bit tricky, though.

When I reached the sidewalk, I stopped, my breaths heavy.

"You okay?" Benji had walked up next to me, the kids waiting a little ways away. I wondered if Benji had asked them to give us a moment. And surprisingly, they had listened. "I didn't mean anything by bringing it up. Tyler had been talking about how the love of his life had seen the error of her ways and had returned for him, and when I discovered it was you he'd been talking about, I couldn't help it."

The corners of my lips twitched up—I forced them back down. I was supposed to still be mad. "Is Tyler even on town council, or were you just trying to get me to his house?"

"Oh, he's on town council, all right. And if our murderer is targeting people that the town wouldn't miss, he'd be right at the top of their list."

"I shouldn't have lost my temper in there. I don't like my kids to see me like that." I paused. "And for the record, I was never pining after you. I wasn't the mistress. And I never stopped to think how people would interpret the three of us hanging out. Sorry if I made trouble for you."

Benji laughed. "No one ever thought that except for Tyler. And that's only because he was jealous."

That made me feel a little better. "Make sure my kids know that."

"Don't worry, I'll set the record straight."

We turned and walked back to the kids.

"Flash. Lilly. I have something I need to clear up with you," Benji said as we approached them.

They watched him expectantly, waiting for the big announcement.

"Your mother was never the third wheel. Tyler was just jealous that she didn't give him the time of day. In fact, I was always the one to invite your mom to come hang out with me and my girlfriends."

"Didn't they mind?" Lilly asked, looking skeptical.

"Sure they did. Couldn't stand it. But it was never any fun unless your mom was there."

I blinked in surprise. "They didn't want me there?" That was the first I'd heard of it.

"Nope."

Lilly looked equally surprised. "My mom was fun?"

Benji released a gunshot laugh. "Yes, very. It was the reason I fell head over heels in love with her. Why I never ended up leaving Amor. Going out to California to pursue a music career only sounded like an adventure if your mom was there. Without her, it would just be a road trip that would likely end in rejection and failure. If I'd gone, I'd probably be one of those people playing in parks with their guitar cases open, trying to decide between buying my next meal or catching a bus back to New Mexico."

I gaped. "You were…"

Lilly turned on me with a shocked gaze. "So, you *were* the mistress."

Flash just grinned. "Nice one, Mom."

.   .   .

I SPEED-WALKED, not knowing where Darci's home was, and assumed that Benji would call me back if I went too far or missed a turn.

"Maddie, wait up," he said, hurrying after me. The kids hung back, looking like they wanted to hear every detail but also weren't sure how much trouble they'd get in if they tried.

"After all these years, you announce that you were in love with me?" I said, refusing to look at him. "In front of my kids? They just suffered through a traumatic divorce."

Benji caught up easily and met my stride. "I know. I'm sorry. I just... I always wondered what it would be like if you returned home. And then one day your mom mentioned your opening a business here, and I was terrified. Would I even recognize you? Would I be angry at you for leaving and never writing me back—"

"You wrote me?"

A pause.

"Every week for the first three months."

I wondered how he'd gotten my address. Whoever had given it to him had gotten it wrong, because I hadn't received a single letter. It made me wonder if things would have turned out differently if I had. I glanced back at Lilly and Flash. Part of me was grateful I'd never received those letters, if it meant I wouldn't have had those two.

"I didn't get them," I said. "I... Let's just pretend the past twenty minutes never happened, okay? I don't want to live in the past—don't want to even visit it."

Benji was quiet for a moment, and I wondered if I'd hurt his feelings. If I had, he quickly recovered by asking, "Not even for Tyler?"

A barking laugh escaped me. Not in the least attractive, but the first genuine laugh I'd had in a long time. "Especially not for Tyler."

And then I caught a flash of auburn hair. A woman was in front of her home, trimming her cactuses.

Benji's gaze followed mine. "That's Darci. Do you think she knows her sister is in jail?"

"We're about to find out."

18

D arci noticed us as we walked up her driveway, and she laid her trimmers on a large rock.

"Hey, I heard you might be popping by," she said, straightening and wiping her forehead with the back of her hand. She turned to me. "You must be Maddie. I stopped by the jail last night, and my sister says you're the best therapist this town never knew they needed. Heard you even humored her by having your session on the floor." She paused. "Thank you. Kandy has gone through so much over the last few years, and I'm not always the listener she needs. Or wants. Thank you for being there for her." Her eyes were sincere.

"You're welcome. Honestly, I've been in a university setting so long, I'd forgotten what it felt like to actually help someone. It was something I needed too."

Darci remained quiet for a beat. "She needs someone

now more than ever. I can't believe the sheriff thinks Kandy killed James—locking her up like that. It's not right."

"I intend to help the sheriff see reason—see that Kandy isn't a threat to anyone," I assured her, though I had no business doing so. It wasn't like I had any control over the situation.

"Darci," Benji said. "I'm sorry for your loss. I know you and James weren't close, but still, he was family."

Darci's expression darkened slightly. "Yes, he was. But you won't find me crying over his death. The way I figure it, there was a reason someone targeted him."

"You're not concerned that you could be next?" I asked. "Could be someone who didn't agree with something you voted in favor of. We really don't know the motivation behind his and Mrs. Bailey's deaths yet. Only that both were on town council and both involved the dining room. Might be coincidence, but I suggest only eating what you prepare yourself and avoiding any parties until Sheriff Potts finds who is responsible."

Darci released a humorless laugh. "If the sheriff is going to find who did this, then we're all in trouble. I heard that she was transferred here because she messed up in the big city. Bad. They didn't want to fire her, so her landing the position here was a punishment. Only consolation was that she got to bring a deputy with her, since we didn't have any. Now, imagine how that makes her feel about our little town."

I knew how unreliable the gossip in this town was, but even so, the narrative fit. And would explain a lot. But the sheriff seemed genuinely interested in finding the killer.

Seemingly reading my thoughts, Darci said, "Why is it that you two are out here warning town council, and the sheriff isn't? Too caught up in paperwork and arresting innocent people, rather than doing anything that is remotely like police work?"

"Unfortunately, paperwork is the majority of police work. But it's not the reason our little vigilante beat me here," someone said.

We all spun to face Sheriff Potts. And she looked livid. Her eyes narrowed, her lips pursed, and her skin tone had darkened to a deep red.

"Just thought we should warn people to be careful, ma'am," Benji said, bowing his head slightly—the epitome of respect. "Not trying to do your job."

The sheriff threw a glance at Lilly and Flash. "Turn the camera off."

Lilly hesitated. I nodded, urging her to follow the instruction. She lowered her phone, but not without a scowl that I'd been on the receiving end of too many times to count.

"I know you all think playing detective is more interesting than your dull everyday lives," Sheriff Potts said. "But there is an actual murderer out there. Someone who has killed two people. And you interfering isn't helping things."

Darci folded her arms across her chest, her eyes now blazing with anger. "Warning someone to be careful isn't treading on your toes, *Sheriff*. It's called being a friend. A good neighbor. I know you don't think much of our little town, but we do care for each other. Something you have yet to learn. And that killer knew exactly what they were doing. Knew Kandy's schedule. Knew she wouldn't be home to get James to a hospital. It also seems that if they had wanted Kandy dead, she would be."

"You know Kandy's schedule," Sheriff Potts said, pulling out a pad of paper. "Tell me, what were you up to between four and six-thirty last night?"

"I was cooking dinner for myself. I'm a nurse at the health clinic and have early mornings, which also means an early bedtime. I never eat later than five p.m."

"So no one can attest to your whereabouts," the sheriff said, making a note.

"Kandy can. She was talking to me on the phone just before she went to the therapy office to see if she could get a last-minute session with Maddie."

The sheriff wrote another quick note in her book. "I'll be checking up on that." She glanced at me. "Kandy was with you last evening?"

What was the sheriff playing at? She knew Kandy had been. We had taken a nice drive to the sheriff's office and talked all about it. Even struck up an unofficial deal of sorts.

Maybe this was us pretending we hadn't. Maybe if we

acted like we'd never talked, the sheriff thought I might be able to get more information from the others. I decided to play along.

"Yes, for about an hour."

Sheriff Potts nodded. "What did you two talk about? Anything to do with someone feeling guilty about a murder they may have committed?"

"How dare you accuse my sweet sister of something so heinous," Darci screeched, taking a threatening step toward the sheriff.

Sheriff Potts looked ready to take her on, though, and Darci seemed to rethink what that would mean.

"My sister doesn't have a mean bone in her body. She'd never hurt anyone," Darci said, her voice shaking.

The sheriff looked at me. "What did you talk about?"

"Sorry, I'm not at liberty to say. Doctor-patient confidentiality."

Darci threw me a look of gratitude. "Glad to see someone in town knows how to do their job."

"Hey," Benji protested. "I fixed your leaky rain gutters, didn't I?"

"Okay. Two people," Darci conceded, and Benji gave a satisfied nod.

Sheriff Potts gave me a look that I couldn't interpret. It almost looked like she was wondering if I'd gotten anything useful out of the interaction. Like just from looking at someone, I could tell if they were guilty or innocent, holding back information or telling the truth.

I gave a small shrug, and she turned her glare up to full wattage, her gaze sweeping over us. Was that part of the act? It could have been my imagination, but I swore that underneath that terrifying glare, she looked almost...sad. And then she nodded to us and got back into her squad car.

"Some nerve," Darci mumbled. "Accusing my sister of murdering her husband. And to my face. I never knew what Kandy saw in James, and I blamed myself for them getting together in the first place." When I raised an eyebrow, she said, "Kandy only met him because she'd come to stay with me after I'd had knee surgery. But the woman loved him. Would do anything for him. Even when he didn't deserve it. She would have stayed with him until his last breath. Which, I guess, she did, didn't she?"

Yes, she had. But it seemed that Kandy hadn't told Darci how bad their home life had been. Honestly, if James hadn't died, I didn't think Kandy would have been able to hold out much longer, based on what she'd told me the previous evening.

I glanced back at the kids, sorry they'd seen the entire heated exchange. They shouldn't have, and if it hadn't been for my meddling mother, they wouldn't have. Lilly had her phone up, recording. I wondered when she'd resumed taking video. Probably the second the sheriff had glanced away and her attention had been on us.

"We better get back," I told them. "The therapy office

isn't going to open itself, and we only have a few days until we're up and running."

"I do appreciate you stopping by," Darci said, taking a step back toward her cactuses.

Benji nodded. "You need anything, you just let us know."

"I just need my sister back."

"And we'll do everything we can to make that happen," I said, once again making empty promises. Sure, we'd do everything we could, but at this point, it wasn't much.

"When it comes time for James's funeral, let me know if you want help," Benji said. "It's tough—a lot of details you haven't ever thought you'd need to worry about, all while recovering from the shock of a death."

Darci gave him a small smile. "Like I said, James and I weren't close. But I suppose I'll need to do it so that Kandy doesn't have to. If I have any questions, I'll be sure to call you. I'm just sorry that you speak from experience. Bridgette was too good for something like that to happen to her."

My head swiveled toward Benji, but he avoided my gaze.

"I appreciate that. And like I said, you just let us know if you need anything."

She nodded. "Will do."

As we turned to leave, a nagging thought kept pressing at me. I knew it probably wasn't the best timing, but it was like an itch that was just out of reach, and I needed to scratch it or it would never stop bothering me. "Darci, I'm sorry. Just one last thing. What were you doing at Debbie's house the night of the party?"

That auburn hair. I knew I had seen it somewhere...the woman who had looked like she was going to join Trish and me when we'd arrived at Debbie's. The one who had recognized me. It had been Kandy's sister.

Darci studied me. "So, you *are* playing detective. Not just checking up on my well-being?" She turned an accusatory glare on Benji, which he in turn gave to me.

I didn't look away. It was a simple question, and I didn't see the problem with asking it. Sure, maybe my timing could have been better. Like not asking right after we had been discussing funeral arrangements, but was there ever a good time for someone to feel like they were being accused of murder?

Darci released a sigh and shook her head. "If you must know, I was making sure my sister made it okay. I drive her around whenever James has the car, which is most of the time. He doesn't like walking, even if it's only a couple of blocks. They were attending the party together, and it's no secret that I didn't trust him. Just wanted to make sure she made it to where she was supposed to be."

"That's a lot of tension you two must have had. You and James, I mean. Did that tension happen before or after you were appointed to town council?"

"It had nothing to do with the council. James and I actually agreed on a lot of town issues. But when I saw how he treated my sister, well, none of that mattered much, did it?" Darci gave Benji a pleading look. "Can I be done with the interrogation session? Please?"

"Yes, we're done," Benji said, grabbing my arm and steering me away. "Anyone else you want to traumatize before we head back home?" he murmured.

I doubted I'd done any damage, but I could admit that my approach could have been a little more delicate. Now that Benji had brought it up, though, there was another stop I wanted to make.

"Just one," I said. "But I better do this one alone."

19

Despite the protests and the whining from my children, I dropped them off at my mom's place, placating them with take-out from the diner. She wasn't any more excited about being left behind than they were, but when I told her I would be doing more walking around town, she suddenly seemed okay with them having a movie afternoon together. As for Lilly and Flash, they felt like I was treating them like small children, as if they couldn't take care of themselves. But I knew if I had taken them home, they would have just left again and followed me as they had when I'd visited James Rodney.

Lilly reminded me that it was because of her video footage that we had seen Kandy sneaking out, though I'd never managed to find out why she had been sneaking out in the first place. But whether my kids had been helpful or not wasn't the point. They shouldn't be involved in something like this.

When I'd finally managed to make it to the town hall, I glanced at my phone. Twelve-thirty. Lunch hour. Several windows were lit from within, though, so I decided to take my chances.

No one was at the security desk in the lobby, so I continued to the elevators and took them to the third floor. A woman with short and spiky black hair was walking down the hall, and she paused when she saw me, a smile lighting up her face.

"Maddie Swallows. I've been wanting to meet you. Been hearing your name all over the place but never had the chance to formally introduce myself." Her pace quickened, and I stuck out my hand to shake hers, but instead found myself enveloped in a tight hug. It wasn't until she pulled back that she took my outstretched hand. "I'm Zoe Flores, the mayor's assistant."

"Oh. Great. Hi." I knew I sounded like an idiot, but my brain was still trying to catch up with what was going on, and apparently speech was the first thing to go when it was overloaded.

"You looking for Sam?" she asked, not seeming at all fazed by my lack of verbal prowess.

I nodded. "Yeah, if he has the time. Just wanted to do some catching up is all. We were friends in high school. I knew Ruby as well, even though she was a bit younger.

Haven't had the chance to see her since coming back to town, though."

Zoe hesitated. "She may not be the same Ruby as when you knew her. I don't know if you heard—"

I didn't want to make Zoe elaborate on Ruby's tragic past. "Yeah, my mom told me. That must have been hard on Sam as well."

"It was, but when Ruby's husband died, and then she had the miscarriage, she changed."

That would do it, especially so soon after their parents had died in that car accident. "It doesn't seem fair, tragedy following someone like that."

Zoe sighed. "No, it doesn't. Don't get me wrong. Ruby is a fighter and has made the best of it. She opened a daycare center to help keep herself busy, which has been a blessing. But she also let her pilot's license lapse and hasn't set foot in a car since that day. Hasn't left Amor at all. Just spends all her time with other people's kids, like that will fill the void."

All of a sudden, I felt bad being here, wanting to talk to Sam about the inner workings of town council and who might have a vendetta. It seemed silly in the scheme of things, when so many others were hurting. I had come to Amor to help people overcome their personal demons, not track down a killer.

But I also knew I wouldn't be able to relax until I knew that the person responsible for two murders was locked up. The real reason I had dropped my kids off at my

mom's? Because I was scared. I didn't want my kids home
by themselves for even a minute. What if they had
recorded the wrong thing? Talked to the wrong person?

It wasn't them that I didn't trust. It was this town.
Things had changed since I'd left two decades earlier, and
this was not the fresh start that I'd been hoping for.

Sam exited an office at that moment, and his face lit up
when he saw me. "Maddie, to what do I owe the pleasure?"

I smiled and hoped it looked genuine. Suddenly I
wanted to be anywhere but here. Anywhere other than in
Amor. That would be the easiest thing—give my kids what
they wanted and move back to the big city. Sure, murders
happened there too. But you didn't suspect your neighbors. Your friends. It was always a faceless stranger.

"Just thought I'd stop in to say hi, but I'm probably
intruding," I said, feeling suddenly self-conscious. "How
about if I stop by when it's more convenient?"

"No, no," Sam said. "Now is perfect. I'm due a break,
anyway. Zoe is always telling me I work too hard. But I
didn't become the mayor just to sit back and hope things
could take care of themselves."

Zoe rolled her eyes, but she was smiling. "The man
thinks he can save the town all by himself. I'm just here to
try to keep up with him and pull back the reins if need be.
Can't save the town if you've run yourself into the
ground."

"Yeah, yeah." Sam gestured toward the office he'd just
exited. "I know it's kind of formal, but would you like to

talk in my office? It has the most comfortable chairs in the building. Even has a couch, if you prefer."

"Sure. Thanks." I followed Sam into his office and slipped into an oversized chair that faced the desk. "You've done well for yourself since I left."

He looked around the office, as if seeing it for the first time. "I suppose, but to be honest, I miss my farm. When I get too stressed out here, that's where I go."

I had nearly forgotten that his family had owned a chile farm. "I'm glad to hear that you didn't sell it when you acquired your position here."

Sam laughed. "I like how you put it. It's better than the truth. I was only voted in because of my dad, and because I wasn't James Rodney. But I'm doing my best to win the town's trust. It's hard nowadays—it's certainly not the place you remember from when we were kids."

"Yeah. What happened? I keep wondering if I made the right decision, dragging my teenagers down here. Now, I worry for their safety. I really want this guy caught, Sam. And your new sheriff... I think she's doing her best. I do. But she seems like she's going through the motions and not actually getting anything accomplished. Sheriff Potts keeps running in circles, asking questions of the same people—people who obviously didn't have anything to do with it, almost like she just needs to appear busy."

Sam rubbed his forehead. "She's a good woman. Complicated. If you hadn't figured it out, being assigned to Amor wasn't her choice. It's also not my story to tell, but suffice it to say, she has incentive to do a good job here, and I truly believe the sheriff is doing the best she can under the circumstances. But small-town politics... It's not something she's used to."

"Tell me about the town council. Is there a reason someone would be targeting them? Or do you think the murderer is just targeting people who they think deserve it? Do you think you could be a target, considering your position?"

Sam leaned back in his chair. "This sounds like you are taking over the sheriff's investigation."

I'd been accused of that a lot lately.

"No. I just want to understand. I have kids, Sam. And they are too curious for their own good. They see these murders as an adventure—a challenge. A puzzle to be solved. I blame their dad for that, but I don't think we can stay if this guy isn't caught soon."

Sam straightened. "I really don't want to see you leave. We need you and your therapy office here. My sister..." His gaze found the window.

"Ruby," I finished for him. "Yes, I heard what happened. I'm really sorry, Sam. No one should ever have to go through something like that."

He gave a little nod. "We've done everything we know how. But if you could talk to her, maybe she would... I don't know. Maybe it would help."

"Does Ruby want help?"

Silence.

I'd seen trauma cases like this before. They wanted the help. Knew they needed it. But were afraid of it. It usually took a long time before I ever saw these folks in my office. Usually they needed to hit rock bottom—become desperate—before they were truly ready for change. Before they were ready to put their past behind them. Because they wanted to move forward, but they didn't want to forget. Didn't want to forget the dead husband. The promises of what might have been.

If only he hadn't gone on that trip.

If only the event had been canceled.

If only I had gone with him as planned, I would have been the one flying the plane.

If only…

"Maddie?"

I started, not realizing I had drifted off into my own thoughts.

I gave him an embarrassed smile. "Sorry. I'm back."

"I was just saying that I do think Ruby wants help. I also think that we might want it a bit more than she does right now. But she does want it."

"She's more than welcome to call and make an appointment. We just opened up the schedule and have plenty of openings."

Sam gave a thoughtful nod. "Can I make an appointment for her?"

I'd seen it done that way too. It didn't usually work out,

and I was left with an empty hour. "If you think she'll come."

I stood, ready to leave. I didn't want to pressure Sam and try to get information from him just because of his position as mayor and the fact that I'd known him a long time ago.

"There's a lot of tension. On the council," he suddenly said, the words bursting out, like he hadn't wanted to say them. "Bickering. In-fighting. It didn't used to be so bad. But every decision is a struggle now. Seemingly simple things that would be overwhelmingly good for the town become month-long discussions, and we don't always reach a consensus. We vote on things, of course, but I know how it will end—it always swings in the same direction. And we've lost out on a lot of good things that way. If a vote isn't required to take action, I avoid it at all costs. To the point that some have accused me of having too much power."

I sat back down. "So, you could be a target."

"Maybe. Except the two people who have died were on the opposite side of things to me. We always clashed, and they always won."

What he was telling me suddenly made sense. "You are a suspect. I was told that Katie was the sheriff's prime suspect, but all the times the sheriff was visiting her, it was about you, wasn't it?"

Sam nodded. "I've said things I didn't mean. There have been times I've been frustrated by the council acting like children, fighting over stupid things. They've single-handedly kept the town from growing and meeting its potential. The homeless community isn't getting the resources they need. The school too. There are people in town who want things to return to how they were thirty years ago and don't see growth as a positive thing. But like it or not, we are growing. We have more people. Fewer homes. Larger classrooms. If we don't adapt, we will find ourselves in an even worse position than we are in right now."

"That explains Sheriff Potts' sudden absence from my life. Just after Mrs. Bailey was killed, the woman wouldn't leave me alone."

Sam released a dry laugh. "I know the feeling." He paused. "I don't know if you've taken a close look at the rest of the town council. But some of them have been just as frustrated as I have at the ineptitude of their council. At their inability to get anything done."

"Frustrated enough to take extreme action?"

Sam hesitated. "Try Hank Peters."

I took out an old receipt from my purse and scribbled his name. "We already stopped by his place to warn him that someone might be targeting the council, but we hadn't considered that the murderer might actually be a member of the council. Anyone else I should pay close attention to?"

"Tyler Baker isn't a pleasant human being, but I don't know that he'd do something like this. Wouldn't hurt to put a little pressure on him and see what he knows, though." Sam paused. "That didn't come out as I intended. I'm not telling you to do anything to Tyler. Just ask questions, that's all."

Poor Sam. Always having to be hypervigilant of everything he said and how it came across. Such was the nature of politics, I supposed.

The thought of having to return to Tyler's place made me want to dry heave, though, so Hank Peters it was.

20

"I'm going in circles," I told Trish, burying my head in my hands. I'd decided it was too late to go visit Hank the previous evening, and I was definitely not going alone. Not if the man was someone Sam could picture as a killer. Angry enough to do something rash.

"Once again, this is not your job. You were not hired to track down murderers and solve the town's problems. That is what Sheriff Potts is for. She has training in things like bad guys."

"I know. But then why does she still have Kandy locked up? And why had she first suspected Sam, of all people? Even if he were a slimy politician, which he's not, it's not like those kind of guys do their own dirty work."

"This one does," Lilly said from behind me.

I turned to find Lilly standing at the foot of the stairs.

Her expression was difficult to decipher, but I could swear I saw tear tracks.

"Are you okay?" I asked, pushing my chair back and jumping from it. "Did something happen?"

Lilly straightened her shirt and patted her hair, as if subconsciously making sure she was put together. "No, I'm fine. Everything's great. Except for your mayor. He's meeting with someone outside of work hours and looking awfully guilty about it."

"Sam wouldn't hurt anyone."

"Then why is he passing someone a suspicious-looking envelope in the background of one of my videos? I was filming last night when we were visiting people, remember?"

I nodded. This wasn't good. If Sam was involved in something, I wouldn't be able to bear it—wouldn't be able to trust a single thing anyone else said. Because if Sam was crooked, the entire town must have been.

"It was when we were leaving Tyler's house," Lilly said. "I'd been pretending to film myself but actually wanted to catch Tyler's place in the background, because, well, he's super sketchy, right? Anyway, the mayor was further down the street. He watched us walk away, then knocked on the door. It wasn't Tyler who answered, though. There'd been someone else there. The mayor handed the guy an envelope, talked for a moment, then hurried away. Guess he figured we were too far away to notice anything."

Interesting that the mayor had mentioned Tyler as

someone I should question. Was that to throw me off his track? Pretend he thought Tyler might be up to something so I wouldn't suspect that he was in on it as well?

"Can I see the video?" I asked Lilly. "I need to see if the stranger is someone I recognize."

She nodded, then took the stairs two at a time and came back with the video just as fast.

Trish watched over my shoulder as I fast-forwarded to where we were walking from the house. I hated to see Sam slinking around like that—he obviously didn't want to be seen, particularly with the envelope that was clutched tightly in his fist.

And the stranger that opened the door?

Hank Peters.

WHAT WAS GOING ON?

Trish insisted on coming as my sidekick, and I didn't have the energy to stop her any more than I had the energy to tell my children that I knew they were following us half a block away.

I was so tired of this. Sick of everyone keeping secrets —lies. Talking behind each other's backs.

Murdering each other.

When I knocked on Tyler's door, it came out as more of a pounding. But I didn't care. I was done with being polite.

No answer.

I pounded again.

Another minute passed before I heard the locks on the door. It creaked open and revealed Tyler, his hair standing on end. He was still in his pajamas—a plain T-shirt with Super Mario flannel bottoms.

"Do you know what time it is?" he grumbled.

Actually, I didn't. I glanced at my phone. 8:15. Not horrible, but generally viewed as too early for houseguests.

"We know about you and Hank Peters. And the money," I said. Of course, that was all we knew. But Tyler didn't need to know that.

His complexion paled. "H-how…"

"I'm a psychologist. It's what I do."

No need to bring my kids into this.

Tyler released a long sigh and opened the door wider. "Come on in."

"Tell us about how this all started," I said, surprised by Tyler's change of demeanor. He didn't seem to be the arrogant guy who'd been hitting on me the previous evening. Instead, he seemed…well, normal. Tired, considering we'd pulled him out of bed, but still—a normal guy that I could strike up a conversation with at the office, or in line at the market.

Tyler scrunched up his nose. "How what started?"

"Your arrangement with the mayor."

I'd thought it had been obvious.

"It really is none of your business," he said, and he really did look genuinely confused as to why I would even be asking about it.

"If Sam is paying you under the table for something, it's the town's business."

Tyler stilled. "What is it that you think the money was for?"

I had no idea. My mind raced to come up with something plausible—I'd hoped Tyler would just tell me. But he'd caught on that I had no clue.

Tyler released a single barking laugh. "Why are you even here?"

Heat rushed into my cheeks. "B-because you are on town council," I stammered. I threw a pleading look to Trish, but she didn't move to speak, only smiled, encouraging me to continue. "And the mayor was seen dropping off an envelope here last night. Hank Peters was also here at the time, which makes me question why he hurried over here after we'd visited him, and why you hid him until we'd left."

"So, you're fishing," Tyler said with a smug nod. It brought back a lot of bad memories, so I decided to bring out the big guns. It was a low blow, but it was all I had left.

"You're right. We don't have anything," I said, to Trish's obvious surprise. "I'll just pass what we do know along to the sheriff and let her sort it out."

That got the reaction I was hoping for. Tyler looked panicked as he said, "Wait a moment there. No one needs to involve the sheriff in this. Nothing illegal is going on."

"Then why was the mayor here?"

"Because I'm about to lose the house," Tyler blurted

out. "Sam said that because I was about to be homeless, he could skim a little off the top of the fund for those living in the park. It was just for one month's mortgage payment. Something to give me some time to get a bigger clientele for my photography business. It's about to take off—I just needed another month."

"What does that have to do with Hank Peters?" Trish asked, her nose scrunched in concentration as she studied Tyler. She was on to something, I could tell. She was wearing her focus face.

Tyler hesitated. "He's my business partner."

I glanced at Trish, whose gaze was still locked onto Tyler. She made the sound of a buzzer when a game show contestant gets a question wrong. "Nope. Try again."

That earned her a glare from our captive audience, but Tyler finally gave in and he folded his arms. "Fine. He's my boyfriend. But no one was supposed to know. That's not something that's widely accepted here in Amor, and if people knew, well, my business would have no hope of succeeding."

"But Mrs. Bailey and James Rodney knew, didn't they? And they used that to get you and Hank to vote how they needed."

Man, I was really starting to hate those two. I felt bad just thinking it, though, all things considered. Murder had a way of doing that.

Tyler nodded.

I wondered why Sam had told me these two might be

worth checking out, considering he must not have wanted anyone to know about him helping Tyler out with the homeless funds. But then I realized it wasn't because he'd wanted to. Sam knew how angry Tyler and Hank must have been. Maybe he worried that one or both of them had done something rash.

"I heard you'd been going around town, playing detective," Tyler said, his lips dipping into a frown. "Told Hank you'd only stopped by our places as a courtesy, but he didn't believe it. Thought you were up to something. Looks like he was right." Tyler paused. "Hank and I—we didn't do it. Can't say what would have happened if we'd been invited to that party Debbie threw. She assured us it wasn't personal—that her table could only fit nine people. Said she was trying to do the impossible and sway Mrs. Bailey and James Rodney in her favor. Now I'm grateful we weren't invited, otherwise we might have been the ones in the sheriff's jail cell, instead of Kandy. She's lucky she was released so quickly. I thought Sheriff Potts was going to hold onto her for good."

I opened my mouth to respond, but I froze. I'd had no idea Kandy had been released. When had that happened?

Trish was watching me, her gaze curious. "What?"

"Her table fit nine people. Someone wasn't at that dinner who was supposed to be. And I think I just figured out who it was."

21

"Y ou need to stay home with Flash today," I told Lilly as I checked all the locks on the windows and doors, making sure they were secure. "Just...stay home. If someone comes to the door, pretend you're not here. Even if you know them. Do you understand?"

Lilly frowned. "You're scaring me, Mom."

I pulled her in for another hug. "I don't mean to. I'm sorry. It's just...this is very important. And you two are the most important things in my life. Promise me, Lilly."

"I promise." But Lilly's voice shook as she said it, and guilt settled in my gut. I shouldn't have gotten involved with this. People knew I'd been out and about, asking around. They knew I had my nose where it shouldn't have been. I'd been warned to let the sheriff take care of it, and I hadn't listened.

I tossed a glance at Trish. "I called my mom. I told her

not to bother coming, that I just wanted to give her a heads up. Which means that she should be here any minute, and with any luck, she's told half the town the latest gossip I threw her way."

"All that in the last five minutes," Trish said, her lips twitching up.

"She probably managed it in two."

I could tell Trish was worried, but in spite of all my insistence on security measures for my family, I surprisingly wasn't. These hadn't been murders of passion. They had been calculated. And the killer didn't have a need to hurt anyone who hadn't deserved it.

One last call to make. The sheriff's line rang. And rang. I touched the red icon to hang up. Looked like she wasn't in the office. Someone had to have her cell number.

Benji.

Nine-thirty and he'd already been out on a job, but he had the info I needed. I immediately called Sheriff Potts, and even though I thought we'd come to an agreement the night Kandy had been arrested, it turned out that she still didn't appreciate my meddling in her case. With all the interrupting to yell at me, I doubted she'd heard a word I'd said. She actually hung up on me.

I tapped my feet impatiently, wondering what was taking my mom so long. I was certain she'd drive, not only because of her extreme dislike for walking but also because she'd be in a hurry.

That was what mothers did. They protected their children. Even if their children said they never wanted to speak to them again. Mothers did what they thought was best anyway. Looked like Lilly wasn't the only daughter who owed their mother an apology, or five. I'd lost count, but I owed my mom a lot.

As expected, my mom showed up at the door less than ten minutes after I'd made the call.

"We're coming with you," Lilly said as soon as I'd stepped outside, leaving my mom and Trish to keep an eye on the kids. Yeah, there was no way my kids were coming with me this time. No one could come. Because if they knew what the plan was, they would try to stop me.

A plan that was full of so many holes, I was bound to fall into one of them.

"No," I said, turning to find the two loves of my life standing on the porch behind me. "The fewer people there, the better." I pulled them both in and kissed the tops of their heads. "The sheriff will be there with me, so no need to worry." I hoped.

And then I jumped in my car and drove away. You never knew when you'd need a getaway car.

MY HEART POUNDED. I shouldn't be here, blindly hoping the sheriff believed me. That she would come in spite of her reservations.

I stopped the car in front of the Rodneys' home. It was quiet. Too cold for the birds. Give it another month, and they'd start appearing. Quail families would run across the road, looking for shelter to hide their young. Even quail felt the need to protect their loved ones. At any cost.

A quick glance told me that I was alone. For now. I hurried up the walk and knocked on the door. No one answered. Another knock.

Silence.

I glanced at my phone. Nearly ten.

Surely it wasn't too early for Kandy.

Unless she had been tipped off.

Which I had been counting on.

I just hadn't thought she'd leave—it wasn't like there was anywhere to run. Not with Sheriff Potts watching her so closely.

That was another thing I was counting on.

"Kandy," I called. "It's me. Maddie. It's really important that I speak to you."

A movement of the blinds to my right. When I glanced their way, they stilled.

I was being watched.

"I just want to talk," I said, knowing full well that she could hear me. "I know what happened at Debbie's party. And the night your husband was murdered."

A pause.

"I can't let you in," a trembling voice answered from the other side of the door. "If you care at all about your family, you'll go home and leave things be."

It sounded less like a threat than a warning. She really

didn't want anything to happen to me or my kids. But she also knew that it was a very real possibility if I didn't turn around and go home. If I didn't stop putting my nose where it shouldn't be.

It was a bit too late for that.

"Please, Kandy. Let me in. I don't want to do this out here, on the street, where everyone can hear. You are in pain, and I want to help you."

Silence.

Then the click of a lock, and the door swung open.

Kandy stood on the other side, still in her pajamas and robe. It wasn't tied, hanging open, like she'd put it on in a hurry. "You shouldn't be here," she whispered, her eyes wide. Frightened.

My gaze traveled over the house, and I listened. It seemed like she was alone.

But not for long. A silver car screeched to a stop in front of the house.

"Don't you say a word," Darci said, jumping from the car. "They can't do anything if you stay quiet."

My palms were wet, my breathing shallow. Darci wore an air of desperation, and that was a scary thing. Far scarier than if she were waving a gun in my face. Desperation made people act in ways they wouldn't normally. It made them rash. Unpredictable.

"She hasn't said anything," I said. "Of course, she didn't need to. Everything I need to know is in her eyes—the pain. The confusion."

Darci's eyes narrowed into slits. "What about the relief that her nightmare is over? What about the gratitude that she can finally move on with her life without having to wait on that insufferable husband of hers day after day? I warned her, you know. But she wouldn't listen. She thought she was in love."

"I was in love," Kandy said, her voice quiet. She wrapped her arms around her waist, as if she could protect herself from what was happening. "And he was a good man. In his own way."

I stood between Kandy and Darci. When I stepped to the side to try to better my position, Darci gave me a look that stopped me in my tracks. "You blame yourself," I told Darci as I glanced outside. No sheriff. "If it hadn't been for you moving here and then having that surgery, she never would have met James. It was your fault she stayed. It was your fault she was miserable."

Kandy's gaze snapped to Darci. "Do you really think that? You couldn't have known. None of this is because of you."

Darci's eyes filled with moisture, but she angrily slapped it away, as if willing herself not to feel the emotions that begged her to take notice. "Of course it is. I didn't have to leave you. Didn't have to move to Amor. I only came because of a special request by the former Mayor Freedman. Felt an obligation to the family. While in California, I'd taken care of his mother-in-law. She was a good woman, and we'd grown close. A short time after her passing, the former Mayor Freedman called and said his wife was sick. Needed a nurse to stay with her. I was the only one he trusted, he said. So I came. After they were both killed in that car accident, the only job I could get was at the clinic. Could have gone home, but I'd grown to love the tightknit community, so I stayed. But this town has changed." Darci looked pleadingly at her sister. "We've all changed. And not for the better. Why didn't you leave with me when I asked you to move back to California last year? We could have started over."

"You wanted me to leave my husband," Kandy said, her words sharp. "The sister I grew up with never would have asked that of me."

Darci looked stunned at her sister's tone. "Because I've never had to protect you—you were always the one who took care of me. But now... I never should have let you go to Debbie's party with him."

"*Let me*," Kandi screeched, near hysterics. "Since when have you been the third member of our marriage? You haven't been protecting me—you've been stifling me."

"You were supposed to be at Debbie's party," I said to Darci, the pieces flying into place. "Everyone kept saying there were eight people at the party that night, but the table was set for nine. All with their own place settings. The sheriff didn't notice because we cleared everything and used the tablecloth to cover Mrs. Bailey."

Kandy turned on her sister. "What did you do, beg for an invite so you could keep an eye on me there too?"

"Which one of you made the puff pastries?" I found the courage to interject. "I know you helped Debbie cook for the party earlier in the day," I said, turning to Kandy. "But I also know the puff pastries were not made at her house. Debbie never knew what they were filled with. You brought them with you. I noticed at the party that even though the filling was concealed, you warned your husband about eating them. Warned him about the cream cheese."

"That's ridiculous," Darci said, speaking for her sister.

"I also know that Darci dropped you off," I continued, as if I hadn't been interrupted. "You couldn't be seen walking around town carrying the murder weapon. It couldn't have been Darci who made them, though. You're the cook in the family, aren't you, Kandy?"

Kandy opened her mouth to reply, but Darci once again answered in her place. "Don't say anything. You simply brought a tray of puff pastries to a dinner party. You didn't know Mrs. Bailey was allergic. You didn't hand her one. Didn't know she'd eat one. Didn't know the pastries would kill her."

Plausible deniability. Kind of brilliant for a murder strategy. I'd have to ask Cameron if any of his research subjects had used that tactic before.

But this had to end now. No more lying. No more secrets. If Amor was going to change and get better, everything had to be out in the open. That was when forgiveness could start. Or justice.

Darci gave her sister a warning look.

"You didn't know they would kill Mrs. Bailey, but you did know she was allergic," I pressed.

Kandy squeezed her eyes shut and shook her head, her expression pained, like she could make this all go away.

"Mrs. Bailey was always exaggerating to get what she wanted," she said, her voice hoarse. "You couldn't believe a word she said. When she said she was deathly allergic to certain foods, I always thought it was a tactic to control the menu at the various town events."

I couldn't tell if Kandy was telling the truth. She seemed to be.

"But you had to know there was a possibility that Mrs. Bailey wasn't lying. That's quite a risk just to be able to have puff pastries at a party. You could have made them at home anytime you wanted. Or made them without green chile."

Kandy wrapped her arms around her waist and was visibly shaking. "I only thought they'd make her sick," she murmured. "A stomachache. Maybe put her in bed for a day. Like what would happen to James when he'd eat dairy. It was meant to be a warning, nothing more."

She paused to take a breath, tears streaming down her cheeks.

Darci glared at her sister. "Stop talking."

For once, Kandy didn't listen. She continued her story, her voice getting higher in pitch, her tone more desperate. "I was tired of Mrs. Bailey being involved in my marriage.

Before she entered it, James and I were happy. I wanted that back. James wouldn't listen when I told him to come clean about that first election. Loved his position on that stupid town council and his mayoral aspirations more than he did me." Her voice softened. "I just wanted James back."

Darci wrapped an arm around Kandy's shoulders and turned her away, like she was going to lead her sister into another room. A fierce type of protection, it seemed. And a way to stop her from saying anything more.

Darci glanced over her shoulder at me. "Have you no decency? Like doctors, aren't psychologists supposed to 'do no harm?' This is a woman who has lost the love of her life. Look at what you've done to her. She's hysterical and doesn't know what she's saying. You should leave now before I call Sheriff Potts and report you for trespassing."

There was no way I was giving this up. I'd never get this close to either of them again. This was it. My only chance.

"You're threatening me with calling the sheriff, when your sister just admitted to bringing the murder weapon to Debbie's party."

Darci whispered something in Kandy's ear, and Kandy slowly made her way upstairs, her body shaking the entire time. Once her sister was out of earshot, Darci turned on me.

"My sister is one of the loveliest people this world has to offer. She is not a murderer. And for you to come in here accusing her—"

"She already admitted that she brought the puff

pastries, knowing that Mrs. Bailey was allergic. Intending to get her sick," I interrupted. "What I don't know is why you were coming to the party early. And why you kept walking instead of joining us. Debbie had asked Trish and me to come thirty minutes earlier than anyone else. What was your intention? Maybe you knew what your sister's plan was, and you were trying to retrieve the pastries before anyone else arrived. You are your sister's protector, after all."

Darci watched me for a minute, and I could practically see the gears spinning—see her trying to figure out if I had an ulterior motive, and how much was too much to tell me.

"I just want to talk—to help in any way I can," I offered, using my most soothing psychologist voice.

After a minute, she released a resigned sigh and gestured for me to follow her into the front room. She slumped onto a couch, but I chose to remain standing. Just in case. Darci seemed to be the type of person to go from zero to sixty in the blink of an eye, and I didn't want to be caught off guard.

"Kandy always uses raspberries in the cream cheese filling. It's her specialty. When I came by the house that morning and saw her adding the green chile, knowing they were for the party, I knew why. I told her not to take them—begged her. But she'd had enough. Said she just wanted to scare Mrs. Bailey a little."

Darci's gaze travelled to the window, almost like she was lost in thought.

"I could have gone to the party. Could have commented on how delicious the green chile pastries were. Could have prevented my sister's attempt to get Mrs. Bailey sick. But I didn't. Deep down, I think I wanted Kandy to go through with it. Was proud of her for finally standing up for herself. I was still going to attend the party, just to keep an eye on things. See how it played out. But then I saw you and your friend. Two psychologists. I'm a terrible poker player, and knew you'd see right through me—see my anxiety. You'd know something was wrong and I'd give away Kandy's entire plan. So I turned around and went back home."

I leaned against the wall, my arms folded. "But how would Mrs. Bailey even know that had been the intention behind getting her sick? It could be seen as simple food poisoning, or a mistake."

"Kandy meant to anonymously text her after the party, warning her that it would be more serious than a simple poisoning if she didn't resign from the town council." Darci paused and glanced at me, her eyes pleading. "I know how this sounds. How this makes Kandy look. But she was fraying—breaking. You must have seen that when you met with her at your office. Amor has broken Kandy, and I wanted nothing more than for her to leave. To get a new start. Before it was too late."

"And you think all this started when Mrs. Bailey started putting pressure on James?"

Darci hesitated. "Yes, I do. It was subtle at first, but then when the former Mayor Freedman died, well, it's spiraled out of control, hasn't it? Sam's a good guy, but he has no control over this town. The council is at the helm of this ship, and Sam's been stuck swabbing the decks, attempting to clean up messes he didn't make. Every time he manages to get one thing taken care of, five more messes appear in its stead. It's a vicious cycle, and Kandy only saw one way out."

"She must have seen that her husband was part of the problem, though."

Darci shook her head sadly. "She swore that it was Mrs. Bailey corrupting him. That he'd been a good person before that woman had entered their lives. Never mind that he'd rigged that first election all on his own, without Mrs. Bailey's help."

A knock on the front door.

Darci's gaze whipped toward the sound.

"Who did you call?" she demanded.

I tried to look surprised, like I didn't know what she was talking about. "I've been here with you the whole time. Haven't had the chance."

Darci jumped to her feet, but I beat her to the door.

"Sheriff Potts. And your deputy. It's about time you showed up. You've been missing out on all the action."

The sheriff didn't look at all amused, her hand on the gun in her holster. "Nope. Been here for the past ten minutes. Might have missed the introductions, but I managed to get the rest of it." She tossed a glance to her deputy. "Be gentle with Kandy."

The deputy nodded and squeezed past Darci and me.

"She's upstairs," I called after him.

Darci turned her gaze on me, her expression livid. Instinctively, I took a step backward toward Sheriff Potts.

"You set us up," Darci said. "My sister doesn't deserve to be in jail. She never intended to kill Mrs. Bailey. And for you to treat her like a murderer—it's unconscionable. Kandy will never recover from this."

"I don't think that is what she'll struggle recovering from," I said, then took another backward step toward the sheriff.

Darci folded her arms over her chest. "What exactly is that supposed to mean?"

Another step toward the sheriff.

"It's the fact that you murdered her husband that will do her in. You suggested she go to therapy to get her out of the house. Afterwards, you told the sheriff the murderer knew Kandy's schedule. Had planned it so that only James would die. But the therapy session was spur of the moment; Kandy didn't have an appointment. I was her alibi—and your opportunity."

And then I hid behind the sheriff, which was a wise choice, seeing as Darci then lunged at me.

Kandy ripped herself from the deputy's grip just as they reached the bottom of the stairs.

"How could you?" Kandy screamed. "Everything I've done was for him."

"Which was the problem," Darci said, spinning toward her sister. "You were never going to leave him. No matter how miserable he made you, you were never going to see him for the horrible person he was. It was my fault you ended up in that situation and my responsibility to rectify it."

Kandy may have been handcuffed, but that woman had a high kick, as evidenced when she managed to reach her sister and knock her out cold.

22

"You shouldn't have done that," Sheriff Potts said as we stood in front of the town hall. I'd just given my statement of what had happened, and the sheriff had walked me out. "That was dangerous and stupid. You said you'd give me information. Not act on it, then assume I'd get there in time to save you from whatever situation you'd gotten yourself into."

"I know," I said. There really wasn't anything else to say. I'd known Kandy wouldn't hurt me, but I hadn't figured out that there were actually two murderers until it was too late. Thankfully my mom's gossip of me having discovered who the murderer was had reached not only Darci, which was why she'd showed up at the Rodneys' home in the first place, but also the sheriff. "But you don't know this town. You don't know the people. You needed someone with a different perspective."

"I had Kandy in my jail cell and was doing just fine, thank you very much. I only released her because I realized she couldn't have been acting alone. Thought she could lead me to her partner in crime."

Oh.

"I'd been told one of your prime suspects was the mayor," I said, "and Sam isn't capable of something like that."

"Neither was Kandy, until she was pushed too hard," Sheriff Potts pointed out.

"Very true."

The sheriff released a long breath. "Do you really think you know this town—these people—Maddie?"

A pit formed in my stomach. "No. I thought returning would feel like coming home. And with my mom popping in at my house every other minute, there have certainly been many flashbacks. But this place isn't the same as when I left. The people aren't the same. That's why I'm here. They need help. The type of help that I think only Trish and I can give them."

Sheriff Potts placed her hands on her hips and nodded, her gaze scanning the street. "They do need your help. But not this kind of work—not the kind of work that has you sneaking behind my back and questioning your neighbors. Leave that part to me. If you can stick to your side of things, and I stick to mine, you might find we can have a useful partnership. We might be able to do a lot of good."

"I won't be able to divulge anything that comes up in therapy sessions. Not unless there is an immediate threat."

"And I won't be able to share anything that might compromise an investigation. But still, you never know."

THE HOUSE WAS quiet when I walked through the front door. That wasn't normal. Not when my mom was there. But then I smelled barbecue wafting in through the back door. As I wound my way through the house, a streak of fur ran past, but then screeched to a halt. Ava.

"You here to get in your daily whack?" I asked, expecting the cat to jump at me. But she didn't. Instead, she meowed, then tilted her head. Like she knew it had been a rough day for me.

I reached out, and she approached me cautiously. After sniffing my hand, Ava rubbed her head against it and purred. "Well, that's a start."

But as if to show me that even though we might be on the road to friendship, she was still the boss, Ava whacked me with her paw and ran outside.

My lips tilted up into a smile, and I followed the sounds of voices. The moment I walked outside, Lilly rushed toward me and wrapped her arms around me in a tight hug, catching me by surprise.

"Mom, I'm sorry."

I stilled. My sixteen-year-old daughter was apologizing

to me? Something terrible must have happened, and I was immediately on high alert.

"What do you have to apologize for?" I asked, trying to keep my tone light.

She pulled back and threw a glance at Trish, who was now very interested in her cuticles.

Oh.

They must have had a talk while I was gone. From the looks of it, something that I would have put a stop to. I prayed that Trish hadn't told Lilly everything that had gone down between her father and me. Frankly, it hadn't been Trish's right to tell Lilly anything at all. If I'd wanted my kids to know, I would have told them.

"It wasn't Trish's fault that I came to her instead of you," Lilly said, immediately coming to my friend's aid. Lilly had always been more perceptive than was good for her. Always noticing things that Flash didn't pay attention to. It made it difficult to keep secrets from Lilly. "I asked to talk to her about it."

Maybe it wasn't what I thought it was.

"Talk about what, exactly?"

Lilly pulled in a long breath. "I always knew that dad was self-absorbed. That you were better off on your own. That didn't make me any less angry that you moved me away from all my friends. But that was why I wanted to go to his place for New Year's Eve. I knew he wouldn't pay attention to me—that I could get away with staying out later and...stuff. It wasn't the type of party I thought it was going to be, though. I mean, I knew there would be drinking and all that, but..." Her voice shook slightly. "It was so much worse. Even when I asked Dad to pick me up early, he never asked why. Wasn't concerned. Just wanted to get back to his burgers and video games with Flash."

"Oh, honey." I pulled Lilly back into a hug. I felt moisture on my neck. Tears. "I'm so sorry you had to go through that alone."

"I went through it alone because you were too absorbed in this murder business to pay attention," Lilly mumbled into my neck. "I thought if we helped you figure out who did it, then you'd pay attention to us again. Like you used to."

My heart sank.

It was official. I was hanging up my detective hat. My kids needed me. The town had a sheriff to do the other stuff.

"It's my turn to apologize," I said. "Sometimes we have to learn things the hard way before we listen to the people who love us most. We won't always agree, but I am here for you. Always. And if there is anyone you need me to beat up for you..."

Lilly laughed as I pulled back. She wiped away a stray tear. "No, thank you. But I appreciate the offer."

I glanced around the yard. At my mom standing over the grill, spatula in hand. She was barking at Benji, telling him that she could handle the meat—that she'd been the one meeting my grilling needs for forty years, and she could handle it for forty more.

She'd be over a hundred at that point, but I had no doubt she'd still be fighting him off with that spatula.

Flash wasn't on his computer, for once. Instead, he had a ball that he was tossing back and forth with Sam. Katie was sitting in a lawn chair nearby, chatting with Trish and Debbie.

Lilly grabbed my hand and tugged me forward. "When we heard what happened at the Rodneys', Grandma decided to throw together this impromptu barbecue. Thought you needed it."

It didn't surprise me that everyone already knew about what had happened. The whole town had probably had all the details before I'd even made it to the police station.

And yes, I did need a barbecue at eleven-thirty on a Wednesday morning. But really, it was something we'd all been needing. Something to help us feel like we belonged. Something to help us feel sane. A way to let us know that we were going to be okay.

EPILOGUE

I didn't know why I was so nervous about this appointment. That wasn't me. I was calm. Personable. Empathetic. I had helped shape countless lives.

But I didn't usually have appointments with friends or family. That had been the understanding in opening this clinic. I would only take appointments with people I didn't have a personal connection with. Trish would handle those.

But Sam had insisted. Said it had to be me who worked with Ruby. Apparently, trust was hard to come by nowadays, and she'd only agreed to come in if it was me she could talk to.

It had taken months to get Ruby to even entertain the idea, let alone come to the office on her own accord. I wondered what had finally made her change her mind.

A knock on the door. Our receptionist, Clarise, poked

her head in and informed me that Ruby had arrived. I asked Clarise to show her in.

I adjusted my blouse, smoothed the wrinkles, and then placed my notebook on the desk in front of me. I repositioned the pen that lay next to it. Maybe I would look more relaxed if I was holding the notebook when she entered.

Before I'd made up my mind, Ruby entered, and I sucked in a shallow breath. I tried to not look surprised by the changes she'd undergone since I'd last seen her twenty years earlier. She was still as pretty as I remembered, but there was an emptiness in her gaze. No, not empty. Hopeless. Like she'd given up. She smiled, as though pretending her life hadn't crashed around her. Like she hadn't lost her parents, then her husband and her unborn child.

Life hadn't been fair to her. She'd lost everything. But I had to give her kudos, because she'd kept going. Trying.

I could see, though, that it hadn't been enough.

"Ruby, it's so good to see you," I said, and I meant it. I wanted to walk around the desk and give her a hug but didn't know if it would come across as unprofessional.

This was why I didn't like working with people I knew —the awkwardness of blurred boundaries.

"Have a seat," I said, gesturing to a sofa on the other side of the room. I picked up my notebook and pen and moved to an oversized chair across from her.

"It's good to see you too," she said, playing with the hem of her shirt. "I feel like I should have been over to say hi—you've already been in town, what, nine months?"

"Yes, about that," I said. "But no need to apologize. I heard that your daycare keeps you busy."

Her gaze dropped, and she gave a little nod. "Yes. Quite busy. And then there was the wedding. And the baby shower I've been helping plan."

"How do you feel about Sam and Katie getting married?"

Ruby's gaze snapped up, and she was immediately defensive. "Katie's wonderful. She truly cares about this town, and she's making a difference. It says a lot that everyone wanted her to run for town council, and she refused. Katie just wants to do good for the sake of doing good." It sounded like a speech Ruby had given many times before.

I didn't move to write anything down, because right now, this was what Sheriff Potts was talking about. People trusted me. They let down their guard. But if I started writing, I knew that Ruby would immediately put up walls.

Silence.

"I'm sorry, I didn't mean to imply otherwise," I said. "I know she's a lovely person, and you're lucky to have her as a sister-in-law. What about the quick pregnancy? That must have been a shock. Was it you who volunteered to plan the baby shower?"

I could immediately tell that this was the trigger. I thought it might be, considering Ruby's miscarriage. She tensed, and moisture filled her eyes, though she seemed to be using every ounce of willpower to keep it from spilling over.

"I suppose they are both getting older, and starting a family quickly makes sense," she said slowly. "I'm throwing the baby shower because I'm the only family that either of them has left. I think. To be honest, I'm still not certain what kind of family Katie has, but none of them were at the wedding. What was I going to do, not throw a shower for my first niece?"

"That was an option."

Ruby shook her head. "Not for me, it wasn't. Besides, I run a daycare. This kind of thing is right up my alley."

I studied Ruby. She was in pain. It was obvious. I didn't like telling people what to do, but rather asked questions to help them come to conclusions on their own. Ruby needed healing, and doing the same thing she'd been doing for the past several years wasn't working.

"Ruby, where do you see yourself in five years?"

For many people outside my therapy office, that question brought contemplation. Excitement. Hope.

But within these walls? Fear.

Ruby, like many of my patients, was terrified she'd be stuck in the same place, doing the same thing. But she didn't know how to break free of the prison she'd built for herself.

"I don't know," she finally said, her voice barely above a whisper.

This time, I did take out a piece of paper—a prescription. I wrote on it, signed it, and handed it to Ruby.

"Do one thing different," she read aloud. "Once a week, any time of day."

"If you are okay with it, I'd like to see you in my office every Friday to report back," I said. "It doesn't matter how large or small the change is. Use a different brand of toothpaste. Get up thirty minutes earlier than you usually do. Take a different bike route to the daycare. Whatever."

Ruby didn't answer right away, but then nodded. "All right. I can do that. I'm not sure how this will help, but I'm willing to give it a try."

I released a breath of relief, having been uncertain if Ruby even wanted to change. Sometimes those who had lost someone were afraid of change, because they were still holding on to that person. And changing felt like they were moving on—like they were forgetting that person.

Ruby had most likely been stuck for the past few years for this very reason.

"I look forward to seeing what you come up with."

RUBY RESCHEDULED OUR NEXT APPOINTMENT. Three times. But one morning, about a month after our first meeting, she burst into my office. "I did something," she said, her breaths coming fast.

"Good." The way she'd said it, though, made me nervous. She had a deer-caught-in-the-headlights look about her. "I'm expecting someone in just a few minutes, but would you like me to set something up for you before your next scheduled appointment?"

Ruby gave a vigorous shake of her head. "I did the baby shower last night. And there's a guy. And it wasn't anything. But then he invited me to go to a hot air balloon festival with him. And I said no. But then I said yes. And there's going to be driving involved. And did I mention there's a guy?"

I stared. "So...you took my advice to do something different—something out of the ordinary. I know that must have been difficult for you. Of course, I hadn't meant for you to start so big, but this could be good for you."

Ruby sank onto the sofa across from me. "No, it's not good. I haven't been outside of Amor for years. Haven't driven in a car. Haven't been alone with a man who makes my heart pound harder than it should. I can't go. But then the baby shower... It unleashed something—I can't leave, but I also can't stay. Not with the way things are. Things have to change—*I* have to change. But I can't do it alone."

"Good thing you'll have this mysterious guy with you, then. You do know him, don't you? You didn't meet him on the internet or anything like that?" A thousand worst-case scenarios ran through my mind.

"He's an old friend from high school," she said. "You actually probably know him. Parker Loveland."

I sat forward. "Didn't you stand him up for a date our senior year?"

A flush of embarrassment crossed her face. "That's neither here nor there. The point is that he doesn't count as my support system for this trip. I need you, Maddie. I'm out of my depth here."

"I'm not quite sure what you expect me to—"

"Come to the balloon festival. Not in the same car as us, of course. That would be weird. But it would make me feel so much better if I knew you were around—you know, just in case I have a panic attack. Or a massive breakdown. Someone to help talk me off the edge." She paused, sucking in a breath. "I don't like living the way I do. I know I need help. But I'm scared. Please."

Clarise knocked on the door and stuck her head in, letting me know my next patient had arrived.

This had been what I'd been afraid of when I'd taken on a friend as a patient. I would never have considered doing something like this for anyone else. But Ruby needed help. This could be her big breakthrough.

"I was always too busy to take the kids to the balloon festival when we lived in Albuquerque," I said, my words coming slowly. "I could ask them." I hadn't guaranteed anything, but Ruby was already smiling like I'd said yes.

"We leave tomorrow morning," she said, already looking like her anxiety had eased. I could tell it wasn't gone completely, but she no longer seemed to be weighed down by it.

"Tomorrow?" I nearly choked out.

Ruby stood. "Your kids are going to love it." And then she was gone.

Yes, my kids would love it, because they'd have to miss school to go. I supposed that if Trish didn't mind hanging back and running things at the office for a few days, I could shift a couple of appointments around.

I couldn't believe I was actually considering this—becoming a traveling therapist. Going on vacation with a patient. Now that I thought about it, I didn't think any money had actually been promised.

Not a patient, I reminded myself. A friend.

That settled it. The kids and I were taking an impromptu road trip. With any luck, Ruby would realize she'd had nothing to worry about, and we'd all have a great time. No emotional breakdowns involved.

Of course, then my mother found out about our travel plans and invited herself, and it was suddenly possible that Ruby wouldn't be the one having the breakdown.

Who did a psychologist go to when they needed therapy themselves?

I had a feeling it wasn't going to take long to find out.

The End

ALSO BY KAT BELLEMORE

BORROWING AMOR

Borrowing Amor

Borrowing Love

Borrowing a Fiancé

Borrowing a Billionaire

Borrowing Kisses

Borrowing Second Chances

STARLIGHT RIDGE

Diving into Love

Resisting Love

Starlight Love

Building on Love

Winning his Love

Returning to Love

ABOUT THE AUTHOR

Kat Bellemore is the author of both the Borrowing Amor small town romance series and the Maddie Swallows cozy mystery series. Deciding to have New Mexico as the setting for these series was an easy choice, considering its amazing sunsets, blue skies and tasty green chile. That, and she currently lives there with her husband and two cute kids. They hope to one day add a dog to the family, but for now, the native animals of the desert will have to do. Though, Kat wouldn't mind ridding the world of scorpions and centipedes. They're just mean.

You can visit Kat at www.kat-bellemore.com.

Made in the USA
Columbia, SC
17 May 2024

35821995R00148